For information address Disney Press, 114 Fifth Avenue, New York, New York 10011-5690.

Printed in Singapore
ISBN 0-7868-0936-1

Visit www.disneybooks.com

Library of Congress Cataloging-in-Publication Data on file
First Edition
1 2 3 4 5 6 7 8 9 10

Written by Maureen Hunter-Bone and Thea Feldman
Global Educational Consultant: Merry M. Merryfield—Professor, Social Studies and Global Education
Created by Editions Play Bac, Paris, France

OUR World

Parents' Note

This comprehensive volume, designed for the inquisitive elementary school adventurer, takes a contemporary look at how children live around the globe. Disney characters serve as guides, introducing, in five chapters, five regions of the world—Africa, Asia/Oceania, Europe, Latin America, and North America. With full–color maps of each region, readers always know where they are, as they journey to a total of thirty-five different countries. At each stop along the way, thanks to vibrant full color photos, kids will learn where and how their peers live. With the inimitable style and humor of beloved, trusted Disney characters, the wide world comes in close and feels accessible and familiar. Kids will get a glimpse of ethnic and cultural backgrounds, the types of communities people live in, the physical landscape of each country, the foods people eat, what kids study, how they play, and key holidays and celebrations, all capped off by one natural, cultural, or historical highlight of each country. Each chapter ends with an offering of even more exciting things happening in each region, including some unique twists on how children around the globe care for pets and celebrate birthdays and other events. A reference volume, as well as a volume that the family can enjoy together, this book will not only whet a children's appetite for knowledge and travel, it will show them just how much they have in common with children living around the globe—proving it is a small world, after all!

Contents

105 Europe

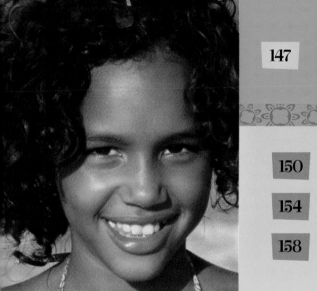

147 Latin America

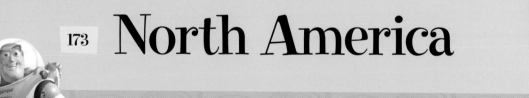

173 North America

Welcome to Our World!

Did you know that you share the planet with more than one and a half billion kids? What on Earth do you think you have in common? Let's check it out!

▲ Ancient cave drawings at Samburu National Reserve, Kenya

Who We Are

We have a lot in common! We are all part of the same human race. Most scientists believe that the first people lived in Africa, and that everyone in the world is descended from them. That doesn't mean we're all the same in the way we think and act! Over hundreds of thousands of years, as people spread over the Earth, they began to look different and develop separate languages, customs, and religious beliefs. Today the world is populated by many diverse ethnic groups—people who share the same traditions and culture. Those who share a culture have similar beliefs, values, practices, traditions, and social behaviors. A culture can include, but is by no means limited to, shared language, celebrations, art, music, ideas, stories, food, clothing, and religion. Thanks to modern means of transportation such as the airplane, people can now travel fairly easily across the globe, taking their culture with them. As a result, they may share a culture yet live very far away from one another! Many countries in our world today are multicultural, populated by a variety of ethnic groups.

Yakety-yak. Kids like to talk—on the playground, in school, on the phone, on the Internet. We can't always understand each other, however. Collectively, we speak at least six thousand different languages! However, two thirds of the world's people speak one of the top fifty languages. The most widely spoken languages are Mandarin Chinese, Spanish, English, Arabic, Bengali, Hindi, Portuguese, Russian, Japanese, German, Wu Chinese, Javanese, Korean, and French. Some of the other 5,950 or so languages are spoken by just a few people. Some tiny villages in the rain forests of Brazil or Indonesia, for example, are tucked away, far from other settlements. Those who live in these villages may only rarely come in contact with people from other places. The languages they speak might not be spoken anywhere else!

> Rafiki knows that we are all one with the universe.

▲ Cell phones are now common around the world.

▲ Cape Town at night

Where We Live

We cover the planet—almost! Of the Earth's seven continents, kids live on all but one: Antarctica. This huge landmass at the southern tip of the Earth is just too cold to have any permanent towns. There are just a few research stations, where about four thousand scientists and other workers live while working on a project. So we spread out across the other six continents, into 193 nations. The continent of Asia has the most people, while the region known as Oceania has the least. More people live near the coasts of continents than at their centers. (If you could see the lights of towns and cities from high above the Earth, you would see that there are big bright clumps near seacoasts or other large bodies of water.) Nine tenths of the world's people live north of the equator, which is where most of the Earth's land is found.

I tell ya Buzz, there's no place like Earth!

We stay close. Most of the world now lives in towns with a population of at least 2,000, while more than half of all people live in cities. And some people live in megacities, with a population of at least 10 million. There are megacities with as many as 34 million people in the center city and its neighboring suburbs! Many of the world's inhabitants move from place to place, either within their own nation or among other nations. More than 2,300,000 kids living in the United States came from other countries. When people move, they bring their own culture with them, but they also learn the beliefs and practices of the place in which they settle. Because people and ideas can now move quickly—thanks to jet planes and the Internet—cultures not only travel around the world, they change as they are influenced by new ideas, products, and ways of thinking.

▲ Pakistani restaurant in London

10

Our Communities

A roof overhead. Most kids who tumble out of bed in the morning—or roll up a futon for the day, or slip out of a hammock—were probably sleeping in a rectangular room. Most homes—no matter where in the world—are made up of box-shaped rooms, with doors and windows to let in light and air. However, in some places, people build round houses; or they dig their homes into hillsides or under the ground; or they live in tents, on boats, or in open-air shelters with thatched roofs.

▲ A Mali man looking out over his field

People live everywhere, from tiny settlements in the countryside to enormous cities. The type of housing they live in depends mainly on the climate and whether they are in a large city or an outlying area. Many kids who reside in large cities live in some kind of apartment building. In the suburbs of cities and in country areas, they are more likely to live in single-family houses. In some parts of the world, a minority of people are still nomads who travel from place to place, bringing their housing with them. Most nomads live in dry desert areas, where they must lead their herds of animals in search of food and water.

▲ Auckland, New Zealand seen from a skyscraper

What We Eat

What don't we eat? Somewhere in the world someone is enjoying snails, roast moth, sea cucumber, stuffed sheep stomach, fungus, soup made from birds' nests, ground goose liver, sour milk, grilled eel, raw fish, live oysters, bee honey, boiled chicken, fermented cabbage, plant roots, maple-tree sap, or sea-urchin eggs. Are any of them your favorites?

Despite the wide range of foods in many places, people usually eat some kind of starch at each meal: bread, cornmeal, rice, pasta, or potatoes. With it, they may have vegetables and meat or fish. The difference is in

the combination of ingredients, spices, and other flavors. As people move from one country to another, they bring their favorite foods with them. In many places today, it is possible to eat popular foods from a variety of cultures.

I'll make sushi out of Sulley's scare record!

Traditional Thai art of cutting vegetables ▶

11

What We Study

▲ *Schoolchildren from England*

School daze. Where do most kids spend their days? In school! They may go to class in an airy classroom in a tiny town in the Tropics, in an old three-story brick building in the middle of a city, or in a modern building wired for computers. They may walk to school—down a path in a rain forest or along crowded city streets. They may ride a school bus or take a high-speed elevated train. When they get to school they learn many of the same subjects: reading and writing, a second language, math, the history of their country, citizenship, music, art, science, and physical education. Many students around the world are taught about religion and morality as part of their studies.

What We Do for Fun

Goal! Sports and games are an important part of life for kids all over the world. All it takes to start many games is a ball—a small rubber one, a basketball, or most commonly of all, a soccer ball. Many kids also play traditional board games like mancala, chess, or dominoes, which are thousands of years old. All around the world, kids also play the latest computer or video games, and, by using the Internet, those who live thousands of miles from each other can play games together.

▲ *Boys playing soccer in Senlis, France*

Rock to the beat. Music is a part of kids' lives everywhere—and with satellite television and the Internet, popular music circles the globe in no time flat. Kids also move to the beat of their own culture. And sometimes they learn to mix styles. So some kids living in Japan have their own version of North American hip-hop music; kids living in Russia may combine Latin American rhythms with their own dance moves; and Indian kids living in London combine traditional Indian music and rock.

Television, books, and movies also cross borders. Kids learn a lot about each other's lives by watching movies and TV shows. The movies and TV shows help move clothing trends and styles around the world in a flash, too.

◀ *Girl absorbed in playing handheld video game*

Schoobie do! I tell you kid, I just love a good party!

An April Fool's Day joke ▲

Celebrations

Party time. People everywhere celebrate birthdays and weddings, observe religious holidays, and mark important days in their country's history. Many countries have harvest festivals and days of thanksgiving. And kids, especially, like to celebrate things such as the end of school, the longest day of the year, and funny events like April Fool's Day (when harmless practical jokes are played on friends), or La Tomatina (a tomato-tossing festival in a city in Spain).

Children trick-or-treating in Halloween costumes ▲

◀ Watching humpback whales—Hervey Bay, Queensland, Australia

Man watering sapling in a tree nursery—Senegal ▶

Taking Care of Our World

The Earth's population keeps growing and taking up more space. All of these people need food and shelter and clothing. They need transportation and schools and jobs. These needs create heavy demands on the planet. People and wildlife often wind up needing the same land, and animals and plants get pushed out of their natural habitats, often with nowhere to go and grow. The world's population is also using Earth's natural resources at an increasingly fast rate. Industry and power plants give off air and water pollution as they work to create products and energy. What can we do to protect wild places and wildlife, reduce pollution, and save resources? In this book you will see how countries and people are working to try to take care of the Earth, our world, our home.

◀ City waste treatment plant Matlavo— Catalunya, Spain.

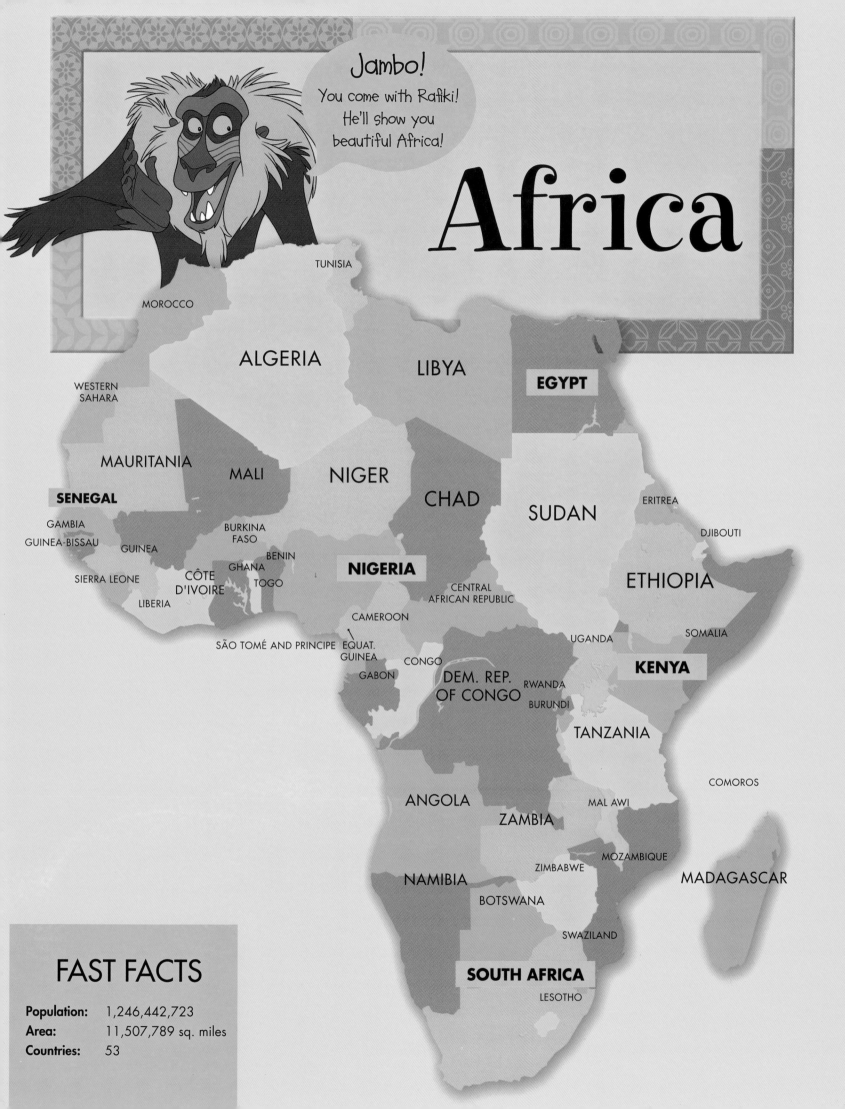

Let's explore Africa!

The second largest continent, Africa is home to people of many colors, religions, and backgrounds. In Africa, you could meet a boy who herds goats in the North African desert, or spend time with an eleven-year-old boy in Nigeria who gets up at dawn to tend his family's vegetable plot before school.

You could watch a teenage cricket player from South Africa, whose grandfather came here from India sixty years ago, or have dinner in the skyscraper apartment of a family in Nairobi, Kenya.

Goats invade this small landing strip in Morocco. ▶

The People

Africans come from many ethnic groups. There are about 800 million people, who speak more than 1,000 languages, spread across the continent. Many are people whose families have made their homes on the continent for thousands of years, while others settled in more recent times. Africa was probably home to the first human beings.

Fossils of ancient humans, 160,000 years old, have turned up in Tanzania. Rock paintings that are at least 40,000 years old have been found in Africa. They show us a picture of the life led by people before written history. About 5,000 years ago, an Egyptian civilization built pyramids and other amazing monuments. Even today's builders would find them a challenge to construct.

More than 2,000 years ago, Greek, Roman, and Phoenician traders brought their cultures to Northern Africa.

About 600 years ago, Europeans explored the coasts of Africa and began settling and colonizing much of the continent. All of these people made Africa what it is today—a continent of diverse people who live in fifty-four different countries.

Two nomads crossing the desert in Tunisia ▶

The Land

When some people think of Africa they imagine a jungle full of crocodiles and snakes. In the lowlands near the equator, Africa has a tropical climate. However, Africa is so big that it has many climates and landforms. It has snowcapped mountains, deserts, grasslands, rolling hills, and green valleys.

On the northern and southern coasts of Africa, the climate is mild, with hot summers and warm winters. In some mountain areas, it can be quite cold. The lowest temperature ever recorded in Africa was –11°F, in the Atlas Mountains of Morocco. The world's longest river, the Nile, is found in Africa. It flows for almost 4,000 miles, from Lake Victoria in Uganda to the Mediterranean Sea in Egypt.

The world's largest desert, the Sahara, is found here, too. The Sahara stretches from west to east along the top third of the continent. Sahara means desert in Arabic. The world's hottest temperature, 136°F, was recorded here.

The climate in the Sahara is so dry that there is usually less than six inches of rainfall a year. On the other hand, the world's second largest rain forest sits on the equator in central Africa. There it may rain more than seven feet a year!

The Suez Canal cuts through the only place where Africa meets the continent of Asia. Africa is bordered on the west by the Atlantic, on the north by the Mediterranean, and on the east by the Red Sea and the Indian Ocean. The Atlantic and Indian Oceans meet at its southern tip.

The Environment

One of Africa's greatest challenges is that its deserts are growing and its rain forests are shrinking. This is due to a long history of exploitation of natural resources and cash crop farming that was begun by colonial powers. Today, there is the additional pressure of an expanding population on the remaining land and other natural resources. Many of the continent's valuable minerals are in some of Africa's most beautiful places. Mining or drilling for them creates drastic changes in the land. The countries of Africa are trying to balance the need to develop these minerals with their goals of protecting the environment.

The Animals

Africa is also home to a huge range of animal life—everything from camels and hippos in the north, to wildebeests and zebras at the equator, to the rare black rhinos of South Africa. And that just scratches the surface!

Animals are a rich part of Africa's heritage. From aardvarks to zebras, Africa has animals that you can't see in the wild anywhere else. It is home to sleek leopards, giant elephants, and rain forest gorillas. There are also tiny termites, colorful birds, and twenty-foot-long snakes. Africa has more than 1,125 species of mammals! Domestic animals such as cows, sheep, and goats are also an important part of African culture. Generation after generation, they have provided families with food, milk, wool, and hides, and a way to make a living.

◄ Giraffes are one of many species of mammals found in Africa.

17

Hi!

Salaam!

Old Rafiki knows, silence is golden.

Egypt

Our nation's motto is Silence and Patience, Liberty, Socialism, Unity.

FAST FACTS

Population:	76,117,421
Area:	386,662 sq. miles
Capital:	Cairo
Language:	Arabic

18

Who Are We?

Egypt is an Arab country. Arabic is the national language, and most Egyptians follow the religion of Islam. Some Egyptians are Coptic Christians, following one of the oldest forms of Christianity. Most Egyptians are Hamites, a group of people who can trace their roots to the time of Abraham in the Bible. Other important groups in Egypt are the Bedouins, Berbers, and Nubians. Bedouins and Berbers used to live as nomads, moving across the desert from oasis to oasis. Now, most have settled down in towns that have grown up around these watering holes. Most Nubians live in the southern part of Egypt. Some Egyptians have roots in Armenia, Greece, France, or Italy.

An Egyptian farmer and his children. Check out the father's galabiyeh. This loose cotton robe is great for staying cool in the Egyptian heat. Looks like the kids prefer Western dress! ▶

▲ *Nubian children play along the banks of the Nile in the small southern Egyptian city of Esna. The land near the river is shaded by trees. Away from the river everything is quite dry.*

Our Country

Three big things to know about Egypt: 1) The longest river in the world, the Nile, runs from north to south; 2) Almost all the land is desert; and 3) Egypt sits on two continents, Africa and Asia. (The Suez Canal, which is a shortcut between the Red Sea and the Mediterranean, separates African Egypt from Asian Egypt.) Egypt has coasts on the Mediterranean and Red Seas. Its neighbors are the Gaza Strip, Israel, Libya, and Sudan. Only the land watered by the Nile is good for farming; the rest is bone-dry desert.

Our Communities

Almost everyone lives near the banks of the Nile River. This is Egypt's major source of fresh water. Small villages line the banks of the Nile throughout Egypt, but half the population crowds into cities. Cairo has the most people— more than seven million—of any city in Africa. Alexandria is an ancient and beautiful city. It was founded about 2,300 years ago and is Egypt's main port on the Mediterranean. Far to the south is the city of Luxor, which is more than 4,000 years old. The rulers of ancient Egypt built palaces and enormous tombs there.

Egyptian cities have everything from wide avenues lined with gleaming skyscrapers to twisting narrow lanes. The cities bustle with business. Egypt is a center for Arabic newspapers and television. Other main industries are textiles, food processing, tourism, petroleum, and natural gas. Four out of every ten Egyptians work in agriculture. The biggest crops are cotton, rice, wheat, sugar, and corn. For most farm families, work is a family affair, and kids are expected to help.

Modern buildings of Alexandria line its shore. The tall, graceful spires in the background are minarets. These towers are used to call Muslims to prayer five times a day. ▼

What We Eat

What's an Egyptian food that's good for breakfast, lunch, or dinner? Most Egyptian kids would say fuul and taamiya. Fuul, fava beans, and taamiya, little fried balls or patties of ground chickpeas, greens, sesame, and spices, can be eaten any time of day! Taamiya is often served in a pocket of pita bread. Egyptians also eat a lot of dates and olives. Other popular dishes include kishk, a soup made with chicken broth, yogurt, and onions, and fatta, a meat soup made with lamb and rice. For dessert, a favorite is koshaf, a mix of prunes, apricots, figs, and raisins in syrup. Of course, in cities and big towns, foods and snacks from all over the world can be found.

Burp! I ate like a pig!

◀ This woman is frying up some taamiya patties for sale.

What We Study

Kids go to school Monday through Thursday, and on Saturdays. They get Friday and Sunday off. (Friday is the holy day of the week for Muslims, and Christians observe Sundays.) Everyone wears a uniform. Schools choose their own uniforms, so the colors and styles change from school to school. Classes are taught in Arabic. In addition to learning reading, mathematics, science, and history, students take religion classes three times a week. Muslim kids study Islam, and Christians learn about their own religion.

◀ These Nubian boys have made models of felluccas, typical sailboats of the Nile River.

▼ Just another Saturday! Kids in their uniforms head for school.

What We Do for Fun

Soccer rules! It is the most popular sport kids play, and also the most popular professional sport. A much older sport takes place in the Sinai desert. Bedouins there sometimes hold camel races. Elsewhere in Egypt, some kids still play an ancient Egyptian game. It's like upside-down London Bridge. Two players sit across from each other. They stretch their arms out to form a low bridge. The rest of the players have to try to jump over it. The players making the bridge try to trap them as they jump!

Holidays and Celebrations

Going to a **moulid** is a big deal for many Egyptian kids. Picture a giant street fair, market, amusement park, and religious feast day rolled into one. Moulids are held in cities and small towns to celebrate both Muslim and Christian holidays, some lasting for several days. At the center of the moulid is a religious celebration at a mosque or church. At the same time, farmers may bring their animals and crops to market. Businesses offer goods of all sorts for sale, and there are plenty of booths selling snacks and drinks. Some moulids feature carnivals and rides and magic shows. Music is everywhere and there is always a busy crush of people.

◀ *A Ferris wheel towers above the crowds at a moulid festival.*

Mystery Builders

Three enormous pyramids stand not far from Cairo, at Giza. The largest is the Great Pyramid. This tomb, which is almost five thousand years old, was built for the Pharaoh Khufu. No one has been able to figure out just how the ancient builders managed to do it. It is about 500 feet high—or the size of one and a half football fields standing end to end. The stones used to build it each weigh two tons. There are more than two million stones in the Pyramid, and each one had to be carefully fitted into place. But the ancient Egyptians did not use wheeled vehicles to carry the stones. They also couldn't use pulleys to drag the stones into place—

the pulley hadn't been invented yet! Records show that it took twenty years to build the Great Pyramid. That may sound like a lot of time. But scientists have figured out that workers would have had to fit a new stone into place on the pyramid every few minutes—around the clock. It doesn't seem possible. But they did it! Sitting near the Great Pyramid is another mystery, the Sphinx. This huge sculpture has the body of a lion and the head of a man. It was probably built to "stand guard" over the tomb of Khufu's son, Khafre. No one knows for sure. The secret of the Sphinx was buried with the people who built it.

◀ *The incredible shrinking pyramid! Over the centuries, the Great Pyramid has gotten shorter. Thieves stole many of the limestone blocks covering the surface, while wind and weather wore away the top. Today the Great Pyramid is 30 feet shorter than when it was finished.*

Hi!

Sawubona!

Kenya

FAST FACTS

Population: 32,021,856
Area: 224,961 sq. miles
Capital: Nairobi
Languages: Kiswahili & English

Our nation's motto is
Pull Together.

We make a good team, Nala!

Who Are We?

It's a good thing Kenyan kids learn two languages in school: English and Kiswahili. That helps them talk to each other, because there are sixty-one languages in Kenya! About seventy different ethnic groups live in Kenya. There are also people of European, Arabic, and Indian ancestry whose families came here generations ago. All of them have had an influence on Kenya.

Kenyan schoolgirl ▶

▲ *Snowcapped Mt. Kilimanjaro, Africa's highest peak, is located in Tanzania, right across the border from Kenya. Many mountain-climbing treks take off from the Kenyan side.*

Our Country

Kenya is in East Africa near the equator. It has a coast on the Indian Ocean. The countries of Somalia, Ethiopia, Sudan, Uganda, and Tanzania border it. Much of the country has a tropical climate, with average temperatures of 57°-99°F (14°-37°C). However, there are highlands in Kenya where there are four mild seasons. The Great Rift, a deep valley running from north to south, is located in the highlands, where the biggest and best Kenyan farms are found. Many of Kenya's people live along the Great Rift Valley, which is also known for its series of beautiful lakes. The largest one, Lake Turkana, is often called the Jade Sea because its waters are the color of that blue-green gem. Kenya's dry, bare plains are in the north. People who live there raise small herds of cattle. Even though it is in the tropics, Kenya also has mountains with snow-covered peaks. Mt. Kenya is the second-tallest mountain in Africa. Kenya is well known for its sizable animal reserves. These are places where wildlife is protected. In one large animal reserve just outside Nairobi, animals such as giraffes, elephants, and rhinos graze in sight of the city.

Our Communities

Most Kenyan kids live in cities, small towns, or rural villages. In the countryside, work is a part of kids' daily lives. They take on duties herding cattle or tending a family farm plot. About one in four Kenyan kids lives in cities like Nairobi, the capital, or Mombasa, a large seaport. City kids live with their families, who work in factories, schools, hospitals, and offices. Kenyan factories produce all sorts of goods: canned and frozen foods, cars, medicines, and fabrics. Some Kenyans work helping tourists who come to see the country's amazing wildlife.

The skyscrapers of Nairobi overlook kids playing by the water in a city park. ▼

23

What We Eat

Kenya is a big country, and favorite foods are different from place to place. Near the ocean people eat a lot of fish. Farther inland, roasted meats such as beef, lamb, and chicken are popular. Corn is an important crop in Kenya, so many foods are made with its products. Ugali are hotcakes made with cornmeal and boiling water. In the cities, foods from many lands can be had. Curries and fried bread called chapatis are popular, for example. American-style fast-food restaurants sell burgers and pizza. And just about everyone loves Kenya's fruit—apples, oranges, mangoes, and bananas.

◄ *A woman grills ugali hotcakes on an outdoor fire.*

What We Study

Students in Kenyan schools have a busy day. They study English and Kiswahili, and they also learn mathematics, geography, history, civics, and science. At the end of eighth grade students take a test to see if they qualify for admission to a secondary school. Some Kenyans then go to a vocational school, while others leave school to help their families by getting jobs. In recent years the schools have tried to teach business and other skills to young people so that if they do not go on to secondary school they will have job-seeking skills. Schools in Kenya fit the climate. In hot areas they have high ceilings, windows, and doorways that are open to the air. Some city schools are air-conditioned. Classrooms often open right out onto the school grounds. Everybody goes to school in a uniform, and each school has its own colors and styles.

These schoolboys wear their uniforms of white shirts with shorts or slacks. ▶

What We Do for Fun

Soccer is the most popular team sport in Kenya. But many a Kenyan girl or boy has dreams of becoming a long-distance runner. Runners are the great sports heroes. Since 1968, Kenya has produced more male champion Olympic long-distance runners than any other country. Now, female runners from Kenya are winning medals around the world, too.

Whee! I love a good race!

◄ *Is he dreaming of Olympic gold? This Kenyan kid gets in some quality running time.*

Holidays and Celebrations

Independence Day—**Jamhuri**—is a day Kenyan kids observe with great pride. The country celebrated its fortieth year of independence in 2003. Kenya has other celebrations that go back many centuries. The Maasai people have ceremonies with dances that last for hours—sometimes even for days. The dances feature amazing high jumps that take place outdoors or in buildings called "jumping huts." Because people of many religions now make their home in Kenya, Christmas (a Christian holiday), Diwali (an Indian festival), and Eid al Fitr (a Muslim holiday) have all become popular celebrations.

The Maasai people celebrate some festivals with amazing jumping dances. Dancers may leap several feet straight into the air—and they may keep it up all day. ▶

Animal Migration

One of the most amazing sights in the world is the great migration that takes place every year from Tanzania to Kenya and back. Millions of wildebeests, zebras, and antelope spend a rainy winter and spring in Tanzania, south of Kenya. The animals graze on rich green grassland. In the late spring, the rains come to an end, and the plains begin to dry up. (The animals have eaten almost all the grass in sight, anyway!)

But to the north, in Kenya, there is rain. The animals sniff the faraway wetness in the air and follow the scent. They form a huge herd and begin a dangerous journey. Along the way, lions and hyenas wait to pounce. As the herds cross rivers, crocodiles attack the weak. The survivors finally reach Kenya, where it is rainy. They stay until the dry season begins, and then begin the long trip back to Tanzania.

▼ *Watch out for crocs! Wildebeests and zebras cross a river during the great migration.*

Hi!

Hello!

Nigeria

You're the best dad ever!

Our nation's motto is Unity and Faith, Peace and Progress.

Who Are We?

Nigerian kids could tell you that their country has the most people of any country in Africa. One of every four Africans is Nigerian! There are hundreds of different ethnic groups here, and many have their own language. In the past, Nigeria was ruled by England. English is still the official language. People from different groups often speak English to each other. In their day-to-day lives people speak the language of their group. Not quite half of all Nigerians are Christian. About half are Muslim. Some people also hold ancient African beliefs.

A crowd of Nigerian children celebrate in the street. ▶

▲ Public transportation is important in Nigeria, especially in its big cities. This is the busy bus station of Nigeria's old capital, Lagos.

Our Country

Nigeria is in West Africa, on the Atlantic Ocean. In spite of its population, Nigeria is not one of Africa's largest countries. It just squeezes into the top third! Nigeria's neighbors are Benin, Niger, Chad, and Cameroon. The Niger River curves through the center of the country. As it nears the Atlantic, it branches out into a number of small rivers. They fan out across the Niger River Delta. This huge triangle of land was formed over millions of years by soil dumped there by the river.

Nigeria has a hot climate. In the south it is tropical—hot and humid almost all year. In the north, near the Sahara Desert, the climate is very dry. In the center, there are rolling hills and plateaus. Due to the higher altitude, the climate there is mild.

Our Communities

Almost one half of all Nigerians live in cities; the rest live in small towns or settlements. Nigeria has at least twenty-four cities with populations of more than 100,000. Abuja has been the capital since 1991. At the time, it was a town of just over 100,000. It was chosen because it was in the center of the country. Now more than two and a half million people live there. Nigeria's old capital was Lagos, a busy port on the Atlantic. With eight million people, it is still Nigeria's most important business center. Another important city is Kano, in the northwest at the edge of the Sahara. Kano is a very old city. It has been a major trading center between the Sahara and southern Africa for centuries. In northern Nigeria, herders raise goats, sheep, and cattle. Farmers tend to live in communities in central and southern Nigeria. Major crops are peanuts, kola nuts, palm nuts, and yams. Oil, which is the country's most important industry, is located on the Niger River Delta. Nigeria is the world's sixth-largest producer of oil.

▼ House painter: this Nigerian woman artist creates a mural on the wall of a house in a country village. She uses paint mixed from natural ingredients like clay.

27

What We Eat

There are many regional cuisines in Nigeria. In some communities, it would be hard to go a week in Nigeria without eating fufu or dodo. Fufu is a dumpling made by mashing up yams or cassava (a starchy root vegetable), rolling it into little balls, and cooking it in broth, soup, or stew. Dodo is golden fried plantain slices. Another popular dish is mafé, which is stewed lamb covered in a spicy peanut sauce. Moin-moin is a fish and bean cake made with ground-up black-eyed peas and chopped fish or shellfish. Moin-moin is often served at special celebrations.

◄ No grill needed: this man cooks strips of meat by arranging them around a hot fire. Street-side stands, where people stop to buy a snack of grilled meat on a skewer, are almost everywhere in Nigeria.

What We Study

Kids in Nigeria go to school all year round. There are three one-month breaks spread through the year. Everyone wears a uniform. School for kids from seven to seventeen is free. Everyone is expected to attend. However, uniforms and school supplies are not free. So some kids have to leave school when their families cannot provide the required uniforms and/or supplies. Many kids stop going to school after the sixth grade and go to work. Students in Nigeria study what kids everywhere study—reading, mathematics, social studies, and science. At the end of the sixth grade, students take a test to see if they can go on to junior secondary school. There is another test for secondary school.

No backpacks for these girls! Some Nigerians can balance homework on their heads. ►

What We Do for Fun

Ayo and **Ludo** are popular board games in Nigeria. Kids also play hide-and-seek and tag games such as "capture the snake." Tagged players join hands to form the snake. The chain of players tries to tag the loose runners until everyone is part of the snake.

Soccer is a very popular sport in Nigeria—especially since Nigeria's national team won a gold medal at the Olympics in 1996! The women's soccer team reached the quarterfinals at the 1999 World Cup and were the African champions in 2003. Kids play soccer in yards and open fields—wherever there is space! Some schools have teams. Basketball is turning into a hot sport to play and to follow. Nigeria also has some famous Olympic runners, so girls and boys sometimes follow those heroes and take up running and other track sports.

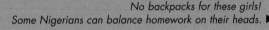

◄ Save! Nigeria's goalie gets ready to put the ball back in play at the 2003 World Cup.

▲ Durbar *riders dash into the town square.*

Holidays and Celebrations

A **durbar** is a sight to see! Picture a crowded town square in a desert town. Suddenly, hundreds of men on horseback parade into the square, dressed in traditional desert robes. Then they swerve, dash away, turn back, and gallop into the square again, coming to a sudden halt in front of the town officials. It's an amazing display of their horsemanship! Many Muslim desert towns celebrate holidays with this kind of horseback show.

In some farming areas, a New Yam festival celebrates the August harvest. Yams are extremely useful foods partly because they keep for a long time. The day before a New Yam festival, old yams from the last year's crop are thrown out. Samples of the new crop are tasted by a village official. Then everyone celebrates. There is music and dancing, and everyone eats dishes made with yams from the fresh new crop.

Children's Day is a special holiday in May just for the kids of Nigeria, while all Nigerians celebrate their independence on October 1. Many other holidays are religious.

▼ *Officials of a town parade in a durbar. Thousands of people come to watch.*

▲ *These workers wrestle with the equipment of an oil rig in the Niger River Delta.*

Now see here, do NOT make a mess of things!

Oil and the Environment

The Niger River Delta is home to many wild animals—hippos, pygmy hippos, manatees, at least 150 types of fish, and many types of birds. The delta is also home to Nigeria's most important industry—oil. From the 1800s to the mid-1900s, palm oil produced on the delta came from crushed palm-tree nuts. It is still a valued crop and goes into soaps and other products. But the delta's big oil "crop" now comes from petroleum drilled from deep underground. About four fifths of Nigeria's oil wells are in the delta.

It's not easy to protect the wildlife of the delta *and* drill for oil. There have been a number of leaks and explosions from oil wells or the pipelines that carry the oil. These accidents are a danger to the wildlife and people who live in the delta. The spilled oil destroys animal homes along the shore and in the water. Explosions have set the forest on fire, destroying the habitats of land animals and birds. Some animals, like the rare pygmy hippo, are endangered. People living in the oil-rich region have protested this environmental destruction for many years.

Hi!

Senegal

FAST FACTS

Population: 10,852,147
Area: 75,749 sq. miles
Capital: Dakar
Languages: French. Wolof, Pular, Jola, and Mandinka are widely spoken.

Our nation's motto is
One People, One Goal,
One Belief.

Stick with me, kid!

Who Are We?

Several groups of people make up the population of Senegal. The largest group is the **Wolof**, and many people all over Senegal speak their language. Other ethnic groups are the **Pular**, **Serer**, **Jola**, and **Mandinka**. The official language is French. (Until 1960, Senegal was a colony of France.) About nine in ten people in Senegal are Muslim. Most of the rest are Christian.

These women live in a beautiful part of Senegal along the Saloum River. Many women in Senegal wear these long, loose dresses. They are stylish and comfortable in the heat. ▶

▲ *The Isle of Goree lies just off the city of Dakar. For about 250 years, the island was a place for holding captive Africans for sale to slave traders from Europe or America. Today, buildings on the island have been turned into museums that tell the history of the slave trade.*

Our Country

Senegal sits where the continent of Africa bulges out into the Atlantic Ocean. This West African country is bordered by Mauritania, Mali, Guinea-Bissau, and Guinea. The long, narrow country of Gambia slices straight into the center of Senegal from the Atlantic, along the Gambia River. Northern Senegal is mostly grassland and desert. The south, near the coast, is tropical and rainy. Most of Senegal is flat, with some low hills. The climate is hot all year. There is no winter or summer. There is a rainy season from May to November and a dry season from December to April. A hot wind, the Harmattan, blows in during the dry season and carries with it fine grit from the Sahara Desert, which creates beautiful red and orange sunsets. One of the most unusual sights in Senegal is Rose Lake, near the coast: minerals in the water make it a bright pink!

Our Communities

Most families in Senegal depend on the land or the sea to make a living. Along the coast, many people are fishermen. Most fish from dugout canoes with small motors. They have to compete against large fishing vessels from Europe. Men and boys do the fishing, and women and girls take care of selling the catch in the local markets. Farming is also important. On most small farms, everyone pitches in, kids included. Peanuts are the biggest farm crop. Other big crops are rice, millet, sorghum, vegetables, and fruit. In the dry north, herders raise cattle.

They must move their herds often to find new pastures and water holes. The bustling cities of Dakar and Saint Louis lie near the coast. Dakar, the capital, is a port where large ships stop for repairs. Most industry is located in Dakar. Saint Louis was built by French settlers. It has shady streets and thick-walled buildings with balconies. Inland, towns and settlements are small and far apart. In these towns, many houses are built from adobe—handmade bricks of mud and straw. Country towns center on a market square and a mosque.

▲ *Second-story balconies look out over the street in Saint Louis.*

What We Eat

The people of Senegal may eat more fish per person than people in any other country except Japan! That's no wonder, because the waters off its coast are full of fish: grouper, barracuda, tuna, monkfish, sole, and carp. A popular dish in Senegal is ceebu jen—a small piece of fish served with rice. Most meals in Senegal include a large serving of grains-rice, millet, or sorghum, served with small amounts of vegetables, and fish, lamb, or beef. Sauces made of peanuts or lemon and onions add some zing. Popular Senegalese soft-drink flavors are baobab fruit, mango, red sorrel, and even rubber tree! Tea is also a favorite drink. In homes, visitors may be served three cups of tea in a row. The first is not sweetened. The second has a bit of sugar. The last is very sweet. The meaning? Friendship takes time to brew and gets sweeter as time goes on.

◄ *This woman is grilling fish for sale on a charcoal grill called a fourniere. These roadside grills are found in many parts of Senegal.*

What We Study

By law, all children in Senegal are supposed to go to grade school. Only a bit more than half of Senegal's kids actually go to school every day. Some kids stay home to help their families farm, fish, or raise cattle. Some schools are too far from home. The government of Senegal is working to bring education to more kids. Children who have missed out on regular schooling sometimes go to "street schools" run by volunteers. These schools can be found in open-air markets, in factories after hours, even under a shade tree in a town square.

▲ *Two Senegalese wrestlers face off in an outdoor sand ring.*

▼ *"Now, class, repeat after me..." A teacher in traditional clothing leads a grade-school class.*

What We Do for Fun

Senegal smackdown! Wrestling is big in this country. Each wrestler usually brings along drummers and singers whose music supports him in the ring of sand. In traditional Senegalese wrestling, when a contestant's back or knee touches the ground, he loses. Another traditional sport in Senegal is dugout-canoe racing. Towns along rivers have their own teams and challenge teams from other towns. And from city parks and schoolyards to the dusty streets of country towns, kids—mostly boys—play soccer. Checkers is also a popular game with kids and adults.

Pinned ya again, Simba!

Upside-Down Tree

Check out the "upside-down tree," the **baobab**. It looks as if a giant pulled it up and stuck it back in the ground roots up. The baobab is the national tree of Senegal—and for good reason. Baobabs are very useful trees. They are incredibly sturdy and can thrive during droughts. They can live for several thousand years, and they store large amounts of water in their trunks. The bark is used to make baskets, rope, and even paper, while the fruit can be mashed and turned into a drink. The leaves, bark, and roots can be used for medicine. In the dry grasslands of Senegal, the trees offer shade to travelers and animals.

Many animals of the grasslands make the baobab home. Vultures and storks make their large nests on the outer branches. Entire families of owls sometimes make their homes in holes in the trunk. Lizards and snakes, scorpions and spiders all find a nook or cranny of their own. A few people have even turned huge hollowed-out baobab trees into homes!

▲ Since so many Senegalese are Muslim, Islamic celebrations are important. Here, Muslims gather outside a famous mosque in Touba.

Holidays and Celebrations

Senegal celebrates its important holidays to a beat—a drumbeat. In many West African countries, drumming is an ancient art that is still important today. Most drums are made by hand, carved from chunks of mahogany or other local wood. The drumheads are made by stretching skins across the top of the drum. A fun celebration for kids is the Muslim New Year, **Tamkharit**. First, families celebrate with a special millet stew served with lamb, vegetables, and tomato sauce. Afterward, kids dress up and go out to entertain the neighbors. Boys disguise themselves as girls and girls dress as boys. Everyone carries a drum—fancy or homemade—and neighbors give the kids candy or other small treats.

◀ A baobab's branches grow from the top of its trunk. They look more like roots than branches!

33

Hi!

Jambo!

South Africa

Our nation's motto is Unity in Diversity.

I'm telling you, this is the good life!

FAST FACTS

Population: 42,718,530
Area: 470,693 sq. miles
Capital: Pretoria
Languages: Afrikaans, English, Ndebele, Pedi, Sotho, Swazi, Tsonga, Tswana, Venda, Xhosa, Zulu

Who Are We?

The first people in South Africa, the **Basarwa**, moved there more than 25,000 years ago. Since then, other groups of people have moved here from central Africa, Portugal, France, Holland, England, islands in the Indian Ocean, and India. All have struggled to learn to share the land. Life was especially hard for black South Africans from 1948 to 1990, when there were laws that separated people by color. Black South Africans were moved to the "reserves" on the worst land.

Only white citizens had full rights. Then, due to the sacrifices of many South Africans—most notably Nelson Mandela—things changed. In 1994, South Africa held an election in which all citizens could vote. Today's kids are growing up in a country with equal rights for all.

South Africa calls itself a rainbow nation. These kids are part of its diverse future. ▶

Our Country

South Africa is at the southern tip of Africa. It is bordered by the Atlantic and Indian Oceans. Neighbors of South Africa include Namibia, Botswana, Mozambique, Zimbabwe, Swaziland, and Lesotho. (South Africa completely surrounds Lesotho.) South Africa is a beautiful country, with thousands of miles of coastline. A ring of mountains sits just inside the coast and edges a high plateau in the center. The country has forests and rich valleys, desert, and grasslands that South Africans call the veld. South Africa is very rich in minerals such as diamonds, gold, platinum, coal, copper, and more. The mild, mostly temperate climate is good for raising many food crops, too.

◀ *Beach houses at one of South Africa's many beaches.*

Our Communities

South Africa is a very modern country, with bustling cities full of skyscrapers, and the latest styles stocked in its stores. Over half of all South Africans live in cities or large towns. The rest live in small country towns and villages. South Africa is also a country in which some people live almost the way people lived thousands of years ago. They graze cattle in the grasslands

at the edge of the desert. And because of South Africa's long years of keeping people separated by color, many South Africans still live in segregated neighborhoods. This is beginning to change.

▼ *Cape Town is the most southern city in Africa. This modern city is tucked between the ocean and a strand of hills and mountains. Famous flat-topped Table Mountain overlooks the city.*

What We Eat

Every group that has come to South Africa has brought its own tastes. All have put their mark on the food. From the Khoi people comes kaiings, a dish made by frying the fat of a sheep's tail and combining it with cabbage. Umqa is a popular pumpkin and cornmeal dish of the Xhosa people. Indians brought curries. Now even some non-Indian foods are spiced with curry flavors. Dutch, or Afrikaaner, South Africans are known for potjies, one-pot dishes that combine veggies and meat or seafood. Another food almost everybody eats is biltong, spicy dried meat strips. Portuguese settlers hundreds of years ago discovered a hot pepper they called peri-peri. They used it to make a hot sauce that South Africans of all backgrounds now use.

Hot off the grill! These grilled foods are part of a South African brai, or barbecue. ▶

What We Study

Here's a question every schoolkid in South Africa knows the answer to: what's for lunch? Peanut butter sandwiches! Every kid in South Africa is supposed to get a free peanut butter sandwich every school day. (Boring? Maybe. But it's nutritious!) What else is the same about school in South Africa? Everyone wears a uniform. What's different? There are eleven official languages spoken in South Africa. Students may choose the language they will be taught in. In third grade they also begin studying a second language. Schools in South Africa range from modern, air-conditioned buildings with computers and plenty of school supplies to small concrete-block schools.

◀ *South Africa has some excellent museums. Lucky schoolkids sometimes get to visit!*

What We Do for Fun

The mild climate makes it easy to spend time outdoors. This is one of the few places in Africa where you can snow ski *and* water ski. South Africa has beautiful beaches along its long coastline. Some of the world's best runners, tennis players, and golfers have come from South Africa over the years. Ball sports are very popular, as well. Almost everybody follows or plays soccer. South Africans of Indian or English background favor cricket, while many Afrikaaners are crazy about rugby football. A traditional sport played by some boys is stick fighting. It's a sport played with two sticks—a short one and a long one. Players lunge with one stick and hold off a challenger with the other.

Kids gather at one of Cape Town's beaches. ▶

Holidays and Celebrations

In 2004, South Africa held a celebration to honor the ten-year anniversary of free elections. As part of the celebration, the government asked everyone to "catch the rhythm of a nation." An ad campaign showcased a special drumbeat. Kids and adults all over the country learned the rhythm. They could catch the beat by snapping fingers, drumming, stomping feet, or clapping hands. The idea was to show that South Africans could join together to celebrate and work together to change the country for the better.

For us, every day is a holiday! Here, Pumbaa! Catch!

◀ Drumming makes celebrating fun!

National Parks

Want to see the big five? They are the elephant, lion, buffalo, rhino, and leopard. These are the wild animals people visiting Africa most want to see. With luck, visitors spot them all in one of South Africa's nature reserves, especially Kruger National Park. This is southern Africa's first game reserve. It was founded in 1898 to protect the country's wild animals, and in 1926 the South African government made the reserve a national park. The only way to hunt the animals of this reserve is with a camera. Visitors can trek through this enormous park to see animals in the wild. Expert guides lead groups into grasslands where they can spot a pride of lions lazing in the sun, or tall-necked giraffes nibbling on the high branches of trees. You might see the blur of a speedy cheetah as it chases down its dinner.

▲ Very lucky visitors might get a peek at the park's prize—a black rhino. There are about 200 of these endangered animals living in Kruger National Park.

◀ Springboks like these and many other animals are a common sight on the roads in South Africa.

Mike's Travel Journal in Africa

Can you find me in the photos?

Salaam from Sharm el Sheik!

Some of the clearest water and most beautiful coral reefs in the world sit right off the shore of this Egyptian city on the Red Sea, at the edge of the Sinai Desert. People come from around the world to check out the amazing underwater sights and also to visit nearby desert villages.

◄ *Sea star from Sharm el Sheik*

Pack up Your Trunk and Visit Kenya's Elephant Caves!

Large underground caves filled with salt deposits attract herds of elephants in western Kenya. The elephants like to lick the salt! Be sure to check out the caves during the day—nighttime is elephant time!

▼ *Here is my cable pass.*

Elephants looking for salt

The Red Sea, Egypt

Take a Cable to the Table!

Want to guess the name of this large, flat-topped mountain overlooking the seacoast city of Cape Town, South Africa? It's called Table Mountain, of course! Take a cable car to the top and feel the car slowly spin as it glides up the mountainside. The spinning is supposed to keep you from getting dizzy!

Cape Town, South Africa

To Timbuktu and Back!

Camel caravans carrying salt bricks from mines in the Sahara Desert still stop in the ancient city of Timbuktu. There the salt bricks are loaded onto riverboats that carry them south for sale. Timbuktu is beautiful, but it is in constant danger of being buried by the strong winds blowing desert sand into the city. People are constantly digging out the buildings!

Timbuktu, Mali

Rescue on the Nile

The beautiful, ancient temples at Abu Simbel look as if they were carved right into a cliff, towering above a huge man-made lake in Egypt. In reality, the temples were moved there less than fifty years ago. When Egypt had a dam built across the Nile in the 1960s, the lake formed by the dam would have buried the temples underwater.

The Smoke That Thunders

Victoria Falls is the most powerful and the widest waterfall in Africa. You can be ten miles away from it and still see the smoky looking mist that rises up from the crashing water. You can also hear the thundering sound of the falling water long before you get there.

Abu Simbel

▼ *Money from Africa with elephant illustrations on it*

Victoria Falls, South Africa

39

If You Lived Here

Home, community, food, school, fun, celebrations, places to visit, and more! Kids all around the world have so many common experiences. Here's how kids in Africa might enjoy a few more things familiar to many kids around the globe—as well as a peek at some unique events!

Happy Birthday!

Sheep and Hyena is a circle game played at parties by kids in **Sudan**. One player, the sheep, goes in the center. The rest of the players try to keep the hyena, another player, from getting through the circle to the sheep.

First, fifth, tenth, fifteenth. These are the most important birthdays for kids in **Nigeria** and a reason for big celebrations!

Okay, I'll sing "Happy Birthday" one more time, but then that's it!

What an Event!

See guys, we can ski without snow!

Many people think of **Morocco** as a hot, dry desert. But you could go snow skiing there! Just visit a ski resort on one of its tall snow-covered mountains.

Attend a race in **South Africa** that calls for contestants to build and race their own boats—which must be made from concrete!

The Family Pet

Coconut milk, goat milk, all milk good!

In the **Congo**, some families have red and white basenji dogs that do not bark. Instead, they yodel when they are happy. When they go out hunting, people put bells around the dogs' necks so they can hear them when they run through the forest.

In **Sierra Leone** and **Liberia** students may give their teacher a special white rooster as a gift. But sometimes the chicken ends up in the pot!

Many Fulani boys in **West Africa** are given their own goat or cow to raise. These animals are kept for their milk or raised for food.

40

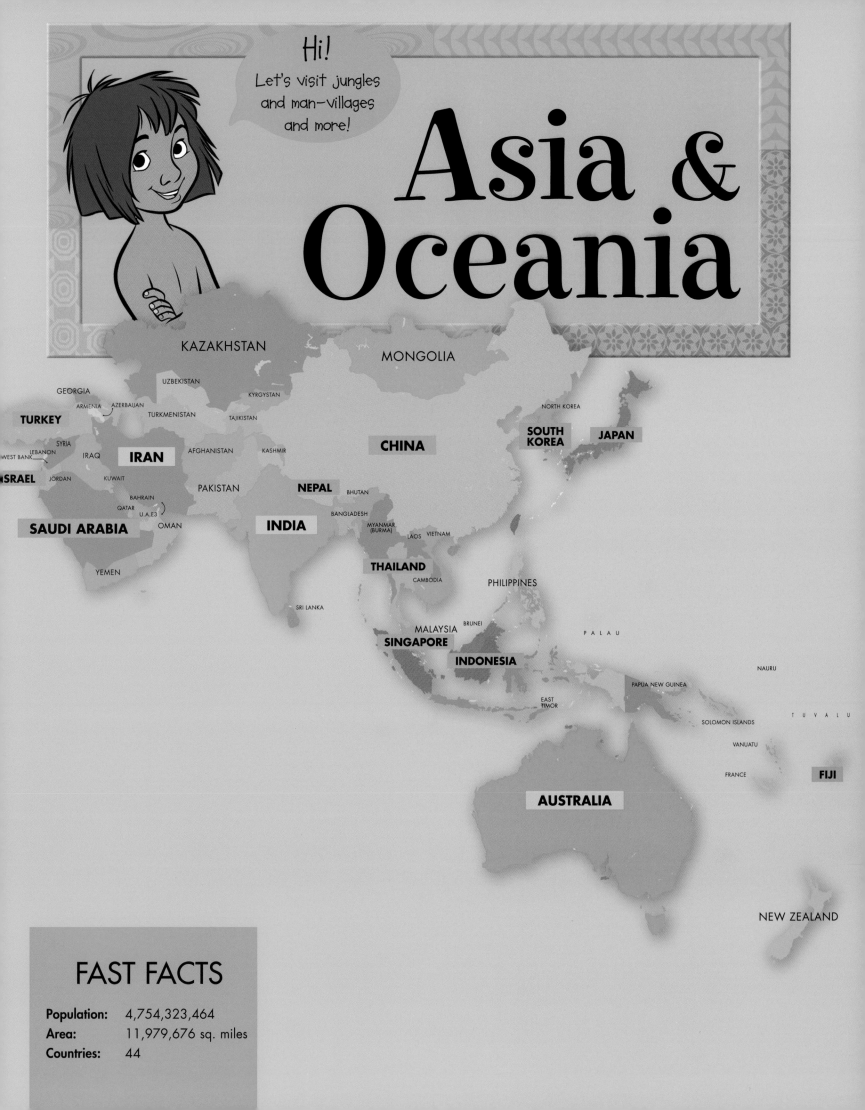

There's sssssooo much to ssssee!

Let's explore
Asia!

What kinds of kids can you meet in Asia? How about a girl who lives in a skyscraper in Singapore? She goes to school on a high-speed commuter train. Or you might meet a ten-year-old Mongolian boy who learned to ride a horse at four. His family has herded horses for generations, but he plans to be an engineer someday.

In Beijing, China, you can meet many kids who are new to the huge city. Their families have moved there from farms to take factory jobs. You might spend time with an eleven-year-old girl in Iran. She goes to an all-girls' school in a small town.

The People

Almost four billion people, 61 percent of the world's population, live in Asia. They live in villages, small and medium–size towns, and some of the largest cities in the world. Singapore, a city-nation in Asia, has more people per square mile than any other country. On the other hand, some interior parts of Asia are very thinly settled, especially the central deserts, high mountains, and plateaus. Most people live in eastern and south-eastern Asia. Altogether, Asians speak thousands of languages. Five of the world's major religions— Buddhism, Christianity, Hinduism, Islam, and Judaism—got their start here. Three of the world's earliest great civilizations arose in the Middle East, India, and China. Over the centuries, these civilizations shared their cultures with the world.

The Moghul, British, Ottoman, Russian, and Japanese empires have ruled parts of Asia. Colonialism has shaped many borders, including those of Iraq and Afghanistan, and influenced people's languages and trade patterns. Some countries have had different names over time. Thailand was once called Siam, and Iran used to be called Persia.

▼ Nepal, Himalaya, Annapurna range mountains in cloud

The Land

The world's highest mountains are found in Asia's Himalayan Mountains. Six of the world's ten longest rivers also run through Asia. The continent has areas that are always covered in ice and snow—and places that have thick, tropical rain forests. (The small country of Nepal has both!) There are deserts, temperate forests, grassy plains, river valleys, and river deltas. Some Asian countries, like Indonesia, the Philippines, and Japan, are chains of islands.

◄ *New Chinatown MRT train station entrance. Singapore's new architecture contrasts with its old-style shop houses.*

The Animals

Enormous Asia is home to many of the world's large mammals. It's the only continent where tigers live in the wild. The snow leopard, sun bear, Asian elephant, orangutan, Ganges river dolphin, and giant panda also call Asia home.

The other thing these animals have in common is that they are all endangered. Asia's growing human population is crowding out many animal habitats as they clear land for homes, timber, and farming.

▼ *Two tigers roaring at each other*

The Environment

Throughout Asia, as in many other places, as the human population grows, the environment suffers from pollution, deforestation, and loss of native plants and animals. The need for sufficient water supplies is critical. China and India, with the largest populations in the world, are among the nations working to alleviate stress on the environment. To curb population growth, China has a one-child per family policy, and enjoys one of the world's fastest growing economies. In India they've learned how to make the soil yield more food through the use of special new grains of rice.

▼ *Chinese workers leaving rice paddy fields in the evening*

◄ *A Vietnamese dad with his daughter on their farm*

Hi!

Nihao!

China

FAST FACTS

Population:	1,298,847,624
Area:	3,705,405 sq. miles
Capital:	Beijing
Languages:	Mandarin, Cantonese

Our country's national anthem is "March of the Volunteers."

Hup, two, three...ooph!

Who Are We?

China has the largest population of any country on the planet. Most Chinese people share the same cultural roots. Nine out of ten Chinese call themselves Han people. However, there are about fifty five smaller groups of people who also live in China, mostly along borders with other countries.

The history of the Chinese people is very long. China's system of writing, which uses pictures and symbols instead of letters, is 3,000 years old. The official Chinese language is Mandarin. About seven out of ten people in China speak it. But there are other Chinese languages. For example, at least 50 million people who live in Hong Kong and southeast China speak Cantonese.

Kids in China are encouraged to join a youth group called the Young Pioneers. They wear red scarves to show they are members. ▶

▲ *On China's small farms, many tasks are still done by hand. Guangxi, Zhaoxing village.*

Our Country

In land area, China is the world's fourth-largest country and the largest country in Asia. It is bigger than the continent of Europe! It has almost every kind of geography you can imagine: snow-capped mountains, deserts, grassy plains and plateaus, wide river valleys, rolling hills, and rain forests. It has many neighbors: Afghanistan, Bhutan, Burma, India, Kazakhstan, Kyrgyzstan, Laos, Mongolia, Nepal, North Korea, Pakistan, Russia, Tajikistan, and Vietnam. China also has just about every climate you can think of, from hot and humid in the south, dry and almost desertlike in the center, to very cold in the north and in the mountains.

Our Communities

Almost forty percent of all Chinese people live in cities. China has many big cities. At least thirty-four have more than one million people. The city of Shanghai alone has more than 13 million! There is really incredible diversity in housing in China—as many different places and ways to live as you can imagine. Some people still live in very traditional communities called **hutongs**, which means "small lanes." These are low buildings grouped around a central courtyard.

Other city people live in apartments called **work-unit buildings**. They share the building with fellow workers from the same factory, office, school, or hospital. Still others live in gleaming, modern skyscrapers. In the countryside of China people live in many different types of small houses, depending on the climate. A typical country house near Beijing, the capital, is made of brick, with two small bedrooms and a central room that is a living room and kitchen combined.

Shanghai is one of China's busiest cities. A new skyscraper seems to go up every week! ▼

45

What We Eat

This huge country has many kinds of food, and everyone uses chopsticks to eat. Most meals include a serving of a starch along with small bits of meat and vegetables. In northern China, the starch is usually wheat noodles or pancakes. In southern and eastern China, it is rice. Favorite meats are lamb, chicken, and duck. Fish is popular, too. In the cold north, people eat spicy dishes made with lamb, like hotpot, where everyone at the table cooks the meal by dunking veggies and thin strips of meat in a pot of boiling broth. Then they dunk the cooked tidbits in spicy sauces made with hot peppers. Many Chinese foods are stir-fried, or cooked quickly in a pan called a wok. How about an oil stick for breakfast? That's fried dough, dunked in soy milk.

◀ A Chinese family eats dinner. Each person selects food from the dishes in the center and eats it with rice in their small bowls.

What We Study

More kids in China study English in school than in all Australian, Canadian, New Zealand, United States, and United Kingdom grade schools combined! The government of China wants all 130 million of its grade-school students to learn English, but they learn other languages as well. Kids in Chinese grade schools have a busy day. They also study Chinese, math, health, art, music, science, and computer skills. Classes in Chinese schools are large; forty to fifty students fill each classroom.

◀ These two boys are concentrating on taking good notes.

What We Do for Fun

Sports are important in China. The most popular are table tennis, soccer, and basketball. However, more and more Chinese kids are participating in other sports, such as swimming, diving, gymnastics, and running, even ice skating and skiing.

Fifteen years ago, it was rare for a Chinese family to own a TV. People would gather with neighbors in a community center to watch television together. Today, especially in cities, more and more people have their own TVs. Kids watch Chinese TV shows and cable shows from other countries. DVDs of foreign TV shows and movies are also popular.

Gulp! I sssseem to have ssswallowed the ball!

Not your ordinary game: in tournaments, table-tennis balls can fly at 125 miles an hour! ▶

▲ Catch the beat! Drums and gongs are the music for the dragon and lion dances.

Holidays and Celebrations

Look out for the fireworks! The New Year is China's most important celebration. It takes place every year in January or February, depending on when the second new moon after December 21 occurs. Just before the holiday, huge numbers of Chinese people get on the move. Many people head to their hometowns to celebrate with their families.

Celebrations include family banquets, exchanging small packets of money for good luck, giving treats of fruit and candy, and watching fireworks and dragon and lion dances. These may last all night!

More fun than scary, ▲ this is the lion's head that leads dancers through the streets at New Year's.

You're more scary without that mask on!

Giant Pandas

Pandas live on the cool mountain slopes of southwestern China, the only country where they are found in the wild. They eat almost nothing but bamboo—and a lot of it, too! A typical panda eats about twenty-two to forty pounds of bamboo every day, and can spend up to sixteen hours a day finding food and eating it. A panda's body does not absorb the nutrients from bamboo very well, so it has to chow down on a lot of the stuff to get the energy it needs.

The places where pandas live and graze for bamboo have been shrinking. People are moving closer to panda habitats. Loggers have cut down bamboo plants in many areas. Sometimes bamboo stands just die off, leaving the pandas with no food. However, the Chinese government has realized that it is important to save these much-loved animals. Chinese scientists are working with researchers from around the world to protect them. Pandas are still endangered, but in 2004 scientists counted them and found that there were about 1,600 of these gentle beasts. That's about 400 more than they expected to find.

Maybe there are some leaves higher up!
Two pandas climb in search of green shoots and leaves. ▼

Hi!

Namaste!

India

Come bring those coconuts here to King Louie!

FAST FACTS

Population: 1,065,070,607
Area: 1,269,369 sq. miles
Capital: New Delhi
Languages: Hindi and English

Our country's national anthem is "Thou art the rulers of the minds of all people."

Who Are We?

There are many groups of people in India, speaking about eighteen major languages. Three quarters of all Indians today are descendants of people who came to India about 2,500 years ago through mountain passes in the Himalayan Mountain range. India had already been home to the Dravidians for about 500 years. About one quarter of the people of India today have Dravidian roots. Although most Indians follow the Hindu religion, one eighth are Muslim, and most of the rest are Christian, Sikh, or Buddhist.

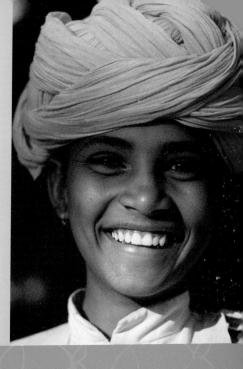

Some Indian men and boys wear turbans, either for religious reasons or for celebrations. In some small towns and villages in the state of Rajasthan, men and boys wear them all the time. The cloth in this turban could be eighty-two feet long! ▶

Our Country

Some Indian kids would tell you that their country was once part of Africa. Scientists believe that millions of years ago the land mass that today is India broke off from the African continent and drifted slowly until it met the Asian continent. India takes up a huge cone-shaped chunk of land that sticks out from the continent of Asia into the Indian Ocean. India is bordered by Pakistan, Nepal, Bhutan, China, Burma, and Bangladesh. In the south, the climate is tropical. In the north, where there are rolling hills and mountain ranges, the climate is temperate.

◀ *Bombay is now called Mumbai. It is one of the most important cities of India.*

Our Communities

Three quarters of India's people live in towns and villages. In most parts of India, farm families do not live right on their farms. They live in small village houses that are often connected to their neighbors' houses. The farm fields surround the village, and the farmers go out every day to work their fields.

The rest of India's people live in big, busy cities. The cities attract people from the countryside because they offer new industrial jobs. India produces many goods: clothing, computer software and services, medicines, and jewelry.

City people live in everything from tiny crowded-together houses to large airy houses and apartments.

Varanasi (Benares) is a very old city with some new sections. The Ganges River, more than 1,500 miles long, flows through many Indian cities. It is used for transportation, irrigation, and drinking water. It is sacred for the Hindus. ▶

What We Eat

India is a huge country, and many different ways of cooking are found in its various regions. Many meals in India are served on a thali, which is a fresh banana leaf or long metal dish. Rice and thin breads are placed in the center of the thali. Little bowls of stewed lentils, chutneys (spicy jams), a vegetable stew, and perhaps a meat or fish dish, are also placed on the thali. Diners dip into the bowls with their fingers, or with pieces of bread or scoops of rice. Some people use spoons and forks. Indian food is famous for its spices. Cooks use turmeric, cinnamon, cumin, pepper, cardamom, cloves, and chilies to make a huge range of dishes with many different tastes. In southern India, coconut is an important ingredient in many dishes. A meal many kids in southern India enjoy is masala dosa, a rice pancake wrapped around curried veggies and served with sauces and chutneys. Fried banana chips are another popular snack. Khulfi is an ice cream dessert popular everywhere.

◄ Chicken stewed with coconut milk and spices is served with fluffy rice and pappadum, a flat bread made with lentil flour.

What We Study

In many Indian schools, the youngest children are taught in the language they speak at home. This could be any one of India's eighteen main languages! However, as they continue in school they also learn Hindi (if they don't already speak it) and English. In small villages, schools may have just one room. Students in all primary grades are taught by one or two teachers. In bigger towns or cities, the schools may be very up-to-date, with computers and lots of books. The school year in India begins in July and ends in April.

Practice makes perfect. These schoolgirls work on their handwriting. ►

What We Do for Fun

Catch a movie! India is the movie capital of the world. More movies are filmed there than anywhere else. Most Indian movies are full of music, dancing, and romance. They often tell old folk tales, but with a modern twist. Many Indian movies are filmed in the city of Mumbai, nicknamed "Bollywood." Mumbai used to be called Bombay. Bollywood is short for "Bombay Hollywood."

The sport of cricket started in England, but India has the most players. It has some of the best players, too. You can see championship games played in stadiums, or watch kids play it in the streets. And if kids are not playing cricket, they are probably kicking a soccer ball around or playing **kabbadi**, the ancient game of tag. On the kabbadi field, each team has a home side. A player runs into the other team's side and tags as many people as possible. The player has to shout "kabbadi, kabbadi" over and over and get home without running out of breath!

◄ Cricket players in their traditional white gear play on a field in the middle of an Indian city.

▲ *Looks like fun: the air is filled with colored powders at the Holi festival, in Bagdaon, to celebrate spring.*

Holidays and Celebrations

Spring fling: **Holi** is a messy festival kids love. All over the country, people do their spring cleaning to prepare. The night before the festival begins, bonfires are lighted, and old leaves and twigs are thrown into the fire. Kids sing and dance around the bonfire. The next morning everyone heads into the streets carrying water balloons filled with colored water or colored powders to throw in the air—and at each other! The colors celebrate the bright harvest to come.

Diwali is an autumn festival of lights, signaling the beginning of winter. Kids get new clothes for the celebration, and families gather for feasts where they exchange candies and sweet pastries. Everyone sets out small oil lamps or candles or strings of holiday lights. The festival ends with a fancy fireworks display.

▲ *This painting shows the Hindu god Krishna and a cow. Hindus consider cows to be sacred. Cows roam free in many Indian cities, and are not allowed to be disturbed or harmed.*

Monsoon

When some people say "monsoon" they imagine drenching rains. But a monsoon is actually a strong, constant wind that changes direction as the seasons change. India has a strong monsoon wind that has a huge effect on the country's crops and on its lifestyle. In the winter, India's monsoon wind is a dry, cool wind that blows down from the mountains in the north. In the spring, the wind changes direction and blows onto the land from the sea. Then it carries moisture from the sea which drops on the land in the form of rain. Some places are very rainy! The wettest spot on Earth is Meghalaya. Some towns in this Indian state get 460 inches of rain a year!

India counts on a strong rainy monsoon to water its crops. In years when the rainy monsoon is weak, crops suffer. There can be a drought that ruins crops. On the other hand, when the rains are very strong, floods cause terrible damage and loss of life. During some monsoons, thousands of people lose their lives. So Indians hope that each year's spring monsoon will bring just the right amount of rain.

Monsoon rains can make everyday life a little harder. These pedicabs have a tough time cycling through a flooded street. ▼

Man, this is one sweet holiday!

51

Hi!

Selamat!

Indonesia

Our nation's motto is
Unity in Diversity.

FAST FACTS

Population: 238,452,952
Area: 741,100 sq. miles
Capital: Jakarta
Languages: Bahasa Indonesia

We'll always be best
friends, Flounder!

Who Are We?

Indonesia has the world's fourth-largest population. Almost nine in ten Indonesians are Muslim, and Indonesia is the world's largest Muslim country. Most of the rest of Indonesia's people are Hindu, Buddhist, or Christian. There are about 500 ethnic groups in Indonesia. The Javanese community is the largest of Indonesia's total population, followed by the Sundanese, Madurese, Minangbakau, Buginese, Batak, and the Balinese. The Dutch controlled the islands that today make up Indonesia for almost 350 years. Indonesia became independent from the Netherlands in 1949. It is now the largest democracy in Southeast Asia.

Some Muslim girls in Indonesia wear long, loose clothing and head scarves. Others dress in jeans or the latest Asian fashions. ▶

Our Country

Indonesia is a tropical country—but it has mountains tall enough to have glaciers! Indonesia is a nation of more than 17,000 islands, the largest island group in the world. People live on about 6,000 of them. The Indonesian islands stretch from the Indian Ocean into the Pacific. Most have a hot, humid, tropical climate. About six tenths of the land is covered in forest.

◀ This woman farmer in Bali wears a long, wrapped sarong skirt and a conical hat to protect her from the strong sun.

Our Communities

Half the people of Indonesia live on just one island, Java. The rest of the islands are much less densely populated. About 12 million people live in Jakarta, the capital of Indonesia, a 450-year-old Javanese city now bursting at the seams with buildings and people. About half of Indonesia's total population lives in urban areas. They work in industries such as petroleum, banking, and textiles. The rest of Indonesia's people live in rural areas.

Many live and work on their own small farms in the countryside. Others work on large plantations. The government has moved some people from Java and other crowded places onto less crowded islands. It cleared huge amounts of land on other islands to create farms, rubber plantations, and coffee, palm oil, and logging operations. More than 6 million people have moved over the last twenty years. However, this shift has created problems, as millions of acres of rain forest have been destroyed, displacing local people.

▼ Jakarta is a very international city. Businesses from all over the world have offices and factories there.

What We Eat

Here's a fruit kids are not likely to have in their school lunch box: the durian. It tastes delicious but smells like a stopped-up drain. It's popular in Indonesia, but because of its smell is not allowed in offices, schools, theaters, or on public transportation!

On most Indonesian islands, rice served with small portions of spiced meat, fish, and vegetables makes up a typical meal. On Irian Jaya and Maluku, most people use yams, breadfruit, and palm flour instead of rice. Indonesia is known for nasi goreng, which is fried rice, and satays, which are strips of meat cooked on skewers and served with a spicy peanut sauce. Rijstaffel is a buffet of spicy sauces, satays, vegetables, and coconut on rice that the Dutch made popular. Krupuk, puffed chips made from ground shrimp paste, is a special treat for kids. Cities and malls feature lots of fast-food places with burgers and pizza, too.

This street vendor specializes in nasi goreng. ▶

What We Study

Kids in Indonesia study a language that is less than one hundred years old. Bahasa Indonesia was developed to give everyone in the country a shared language. Indonesians collectively speak about 300 languages! The school day in Indonesia also includes lessons in English, history, geography, science, math, art, and physical education.

◀ *Sharing secrets: girls chat while waiting for school to begin. Their uniform shirts carry their school's crest on the pocket.*

▲ *Building and flying spectacular kites is a hobby in Indonesia, especially on the island of Bali.*

What We Do for Fun

Land of the speeding shuttlecock: some of the best badminton players in the world come from Indonesia. Other popular sports include soccer, swimming, volleyball, and basketball. **Pencak Silat** is a fighting sport a bit like judo or karate. Chess is a popular game, especially in the northern islands. Many city kids also play computer games and like to watch TV.

Volley: this badminton player takes aim at the feathered shuttlecock. ▶

Holidays and Celebrations

Muslims, Hindus, Buddhists, and Christians each celebrate their own religious holidays. One holiday everybody celebrates in a big way is Independence Day, August 17. The whole country spends several weeks getting ready for the big day. Neighborhoods hold cleanups, and some people even repaint their houses. On August 17 there are parades in the capital and celebrations all over the country. A part of many neighborhood and city celebrations is **Panjat Pinang**, a palm-tree-climbing contest. A tall, palm tree trunk is greased, and prizes are hung from the top. The prizes include everything from small toys to TV sets and bicycles. Climbers have to reach the top to claim a prize. Kids and adults alike give it a try!

If I lived on land, I'd climb trees every day!

Muslim women praying during Eid-el-Fithr celebration ▲

Losing the Forest

About six tenths of Indonesia's land is rain forest. Imagine walking into one of these forests. The air is very damp and warm. You look up and the branches of the trees are so thick that only tiny portions of sky peep through. Watch your step! Twisted roots of trees and vines make the forest floor hard to walk on. You wear long-sleeved shirts and long pants and have used a lot of insect repellent. There are so many buzzing insects! From time to time you see a spectacular butterfly. If you are really lucky, you may catch a glimpse of a tiger or a shaggy, orange-haired orangutan. Ten years ago, there were 12,000 of these primates living in one Indonesian rain forest. Today, there are fewer than 4,000.

▲ Piles of logs are ready for shipment to countries far away from Indonesia.

Indonesia is rapidly losing its forests. Each year, about 5 million acres are lost. Most of this is from logging for timber, or from enormous forest fires as farmers clear the land to plant crops. Mining companies, oil companies, and large agricultural businesses also cut down forests for their operations. As people move from Java and other crowded areas to forest areas, the trees are cleared to make room for them. Some of the clearing of forests is illegal—farmers aren't supposed to clear land by setting fires, and loggers are prohibited from cutting down trees in protected areas. In other cases, however, the government allows the clearing, as it is trying to balance the needs of companies and farmers with the value of preserving primary forests.

The loss of the forest creates many serious problems. These include the washing away of soil on the forest floor which leads to flooding, and the loss of homes for some of Indonesia's already endangered wildlife, such as tigers, elephants, and orangutans. We also depend on rain forests to clean the air, so the potential loss of the Indonesian rain forest is a problem shared by the whole world.

Hi!

Sal'am!

This place is home sssssweet home!

Iran

FAST FACTS

Population:	69,018,924
Area:	636,308 sq. miles
Capital:	Tehran
Languages:	Farsi

Our country's national anthem is "National Anthem of the Islamic Republic of Iran."

Who Are We?

Iranians are descendants of many different ethnic groups who settled here over many centuries. The largest group are Persians, who make up more than half the population. Other groups came from central Asia, the Indian subcontinent, or the Arabian Peninsula. Almost all Iranians are Muslim. Less than one percent are Christian, Zoroastrian (an ancient Persian religion), Baha'i, or Jewish.

How about a treat of some fresh fish eggs? This man works in Iran's caviar industry, harvesting eggs from sturgeon in the Caspian Sea. ▶

Our Country

Iran is a Middle Eastern country in the southwestern part of Asia. It borders the Gulf of Oman, the Caspian Sea, and the Persian Gulf. Its neighbors are Pakistan, Afghanistan, Armenia, Azerbaijan, Iraq, Turkey, and Turkmenistan. It has mountain ranges and a high, flat central area. It is very dry, and part of the land is desert. Most of Iran has very cold winters and very hot summers. The country is rich in oil, which it produces and sells to many other countries. Farmers raise wheat, sugar beets, and many kinds of fruits. Iran is known for its melons. Iran is also famous for fabrics and for beautiful handwoven carpets.

▲ *Farmers grow rice on terraced fields, called paddies, in the fertile Sharak valley.*

Our Communities

About six in ten Iranians live in cities. The rest live in towns and small settlements. Some Iranians are nomadic herders, moving with their sheep or cattle to find pasture and water. Many of Iran's cities have sections that are very old. Ancient mosques and courtyards are sometimes surrounded by modern factories, shops, and apartment blocks. In the countryside, many people live in houses made of mud bricks and wooden beams. In one mountain town, Masooleh, the houses are built up the slope of the mountain, one behind the other. The roof of each lower house becomes the yard for the one above!

This man in Western clothes bicycles past women wearing the chador, a garment that covers them and is supposed to protect their modesty. ▶

What We Eat

Looking for fast food in Iran? Try a kebab from a street vendor. These are chunks of meat cooked on a skewer. Dolme-ye, grape leaves stuffed with spiced rice, is another quick treat. Try a cool yogurt drink or some fruit juice. Most meals in Iran are based on a large portion of rice. The rice is often flavored with ingredients like parsley, dill, raisins, currants, pomegranates, nuts, garlic, saffron, or cinnamon. It's served with small amounts of lamb or chicken and vegetables such as cabbage, eggplant, and spinach. Some popular fruits in Iran are figs, apricots, pomegranates, and peaches. Pistachio nuts are a snack food found everywhere.

◄ This family gathers for a meal, sitting on the floor around a low table.

What We Study

Boys and girls never tease each other in Iranian schools. Why? Usually boys and girls don't attend school together. When most girls are about nine years old, they must stay away from boys and wear scarves—**hijabs**—that cover their hair, and loose coats or jackets when they are on the way to school or out in public. These practices are cultural as well as religious and have changed over time to more or less conservative norms.

Kids have to go to school from age six to eleven. After that, they must pass a test to go on to middle school, and another to go on to high school. In school they study reading and writing, history, math, science, and Islam.

No girls allowed! Boys and girls go to separate schools in Iran. ▶

What We Do for Fun

Boys and girls take part in many sports in Iran, but they play separately. Girls learn soccer, karate, archery, swimming, and other sports, but compete only with other girls. They usually play indoors and have women coaches and officials.

Nose and Ear is a silly Iranian game that lots of kids enjoy. You get a bunch of kids in a circle and choose a leader. Then the leader pats the head or pulls the ear or nose of the player to the right, who must repeat the action. Each player around the circle repeats the action, and anyone who laughs or messes up is out. The leader then tries another tug, or makes a funny face or says something silly, and it goes all around the circle again. This keeps up until only one person is left.

◄ Girls enjoy a ride on a giant slide.

Holidays and Celebrations

Noruz started out as a festival celebrated in the Zoroastrian religion, but now all Iranians celebrate it. It is the Persian New Year. Kids look forward to the spring festival because it's really fun, and because they get new clothes in order to start the New Year fresh. Getting ready for Noruz starts a couple of weeks early. Iranians clean their houses from top to bottom. This is called **Khaneh Tekani**. It means "shaking the house!" On the eve of the Wednesday before Noruz, people build small bonfires outdoors. Everybody takes turns jumping over the fire. This is supposed to bring good luck for the New Year, since it burns up all the bad luck and leftover rubbish that needs to be swept away. Then kids bring in the New Year with a bang. They run around the neighborhood in disguise, banging on pots and pans. Neighbors give them treats.

One of the most important festivals in the Muslim year is the end of Ramadan, the last day people share a sacrifice meal. ▶

Colored Tiles

Many of Iran's most beautiful mosques and palaces were built more than 500 years ago. The mosques had enormous inner rooms, high domes, elegant spires, courtyards, and pillars. The Persian builders covered many of the walls, domes, and spires in complicated designs made of small glazed tiles. By tradition, the designs on the walls and domes were geometric. This showed the artist's interest in mathematics. Many Islamic philosophers believed that the universe could be understood with mathematics. Creating designs that depended on geometry was a way of showing God's design. Also, Islamic art almost never uses pictures of people or animals. It is considered wrong to try to show the image of a living being. Islamic tile designs are complex, repeating patterns of curves and rectangles and words.

◀ *Bluer than the sky. The amazing blue and turquoise colors of so many domes come from glazes made with copper. The patterns of this dome hold a viewer's attention!*

Hi!

Shalom!

Just keep on hoping and you'll be as big as Colonel Hathi someday!

Israel

FAST FACTS

Population: 6,199,008
Area: 8,019 sq. miles
Capital: Jerusalem
Languages: Hebrew, Arabic

Our country's national anthem is "The Hope."

Who Are We?

Israel is a young country, founded in 1948 by the United Nations, who wanted Jews to have a homeland after the horrors of the Holocaust. About six in ten people in Israel trace their roots to Europe, Asia, the Americas, or Africa. Israelis come from at least eighty other countries. Eight out of ten people in Israel are Jewish. Others are Palestinian Christians or Muslims. Hebrew is the official language, but many people also speak English or Arabic.

Like families around the world, many Israeli families are close. ▶

Our Country

Israel is so small a jet could fly across the entire country in six minutes! Yet it has snow-capped mountains, a desert, forests, beautiful beaches, and an inland sea. This small country sits on the Arabian Peninsula. It is bordered on the west by the Mediterranean Sea. Its neighbors are Gaza, Egypt, Jordan, the West Bank, Lebanon, and Syria. Israel also has a small port, Eilat, on the Gulf of Aqaba.

◀ *Jaffa, the oldest port in Israel, is still a busy port today.*

Our Communities

Modern Israeli kids can walk along busy streets that were busy in biblical times, too. The capital city of Jerusalem goes back at least 5,000 years. Nazareth and Caesaria were bustling towns when ancient Roman emperors ruled. People have lived in the desert town of Bet Shean for more than 6,000 years. Israel is full of new cities and towns, too. The large city of Tel Aviv, on the shores of the Mediterranean Sea is less than one hundred years old. Some Israeli kids grow up on a kibbutz. A kibbutz is a settlement that is owned by the group that lives on it. In many cases, even the houses are owned by the group instead of by individual families. The kibbutz runs its own schools, medical clinics, and businesses. Members of the kibbutz share in the work, and all share in the profits. There are about 250 kibbutzim in Israel.

Nice day for a walk. This street in a typical Israeli town has been turned into a walkway. No cars allowed! In older Israeli cities, some streets date back to biblical times and are much too narrow for cars to pass through. ▶

61

What We Eat

Because so many Israelis have roots in other countries, you can get just about any kind of food you might like in Israel. There are favorite Israeli-style foods, however. Megadarra is a soup made with rice and lentils. Sabich is breakfast in a pita pocket. It's made with fried eggplant, hummus, steamed potatoes, hard-boiled egg, salad greens, and mango pickle. Many Israeli meals feature fish or lamb, grains like couscous, bulghur wheat or lentils, and vegetables and fruits like olives, avocado, grapes, figs, eggplant, and citrus fruits.

◄ Open-air vendors sell lots of treats, such as these sesame bread twists.

What We Study

There are many different types of public schools in Israel. Jewish kids attend state schools or state religious schools. Most Arab kids go to Muslim schools. Israel is a country of newcomers. Kids moving to Israel from other countries may not speak the official language, Hebrew. So new kids get special lessons in Hebrew and Israeli history so they can catch up to their classmates.

This Arab Israeli girl gets some help with her schoolwork at home. ▶

What We Do for Fun

Swimming—in lakes, pools, or at the beach–is Israel's most popular sport. Matkot is a cross between tennis and paddle ball. There's at least one game going on at every Israeli beach. Lots of kids also play soccer or basketball. Tennis centers have been set up across the country, so more and more kids are learning to play.

Board games like chess, checkers, and **shesh besh**—a kind of backgammon—are hits with Israeli kids and adults alike.

This is the life, ain't it, kid?

◄ A camping trip by camel is an exciting way to discover the Eilat mountains.

62

Holidays and Celebrations

▲ Independence Day parade.

Purim is the favorite holiday of many Israeli kids. They get to dress up in costumes and make a racket with a special noisemaker called a gragger! It's all part of a holiday that commemorates an ancient Jewish queen's victory over Hamman, an evil official who threatened her people.

Independence Day, in the spring, is another favorite holiday for most kids and adults. There are parades and fireworks and barbecues. And there is a silly tradition of bonking each other on the head with joke plastic hammers that make a squeaky noise.

Kids in Israel dress up in all sorts of costumes for Purim. ▶

Dead Sea

They call it the Dead Sea for a reason. Not a single thing can live in it! The Dead Sea is so salty that it is poisonous to any fish or bird that might come in contact with it. No plants grow in this sea, but people can swim in it without harm. This amazing place is located in between Israel and Jordan. The Dead Sea is a fifty-mile-long body of water that sits 1,340 feet below the level of the sea. That makes it the lowest body of water in the world. It is quite deep, too—2,000 feet below sea level at its deepest part. How did this inland sea get so salty? A river of fresh water carries minerals and salts into the Dead Sea. Then some of the fresh water evaporates into the desert air, leaving the minerals and salts behind. There are no rivers leading out of the Dead Sea that would carry minerals away, so they are trapped. Over thousands of years, the minerals have collected in the waters of the Dead Sea. The surface water is salty, but a visit to the bottom of the sea would shrivel you up! A heavy deposit of salts and chemicals have sunk to the bottom over the centuries.

◀ *It floats your boat, and you, too! The extra-salty water of the Dead Sea makes it impossible for anyone to sink—even a nonswimmer floats easily.*

Hi!

Konnichi wa!

Look, man cub!
It's the man village!

Japan

Our country's national anthem is "The Emperor's Reign."

FAST FACTS

Population: 127,333,002
Area: 145,883 sq. miles
Capital: Tokyo
Languages: Japanese

Who Are We?

Japan is not a diverse country: almost all of Japan's 127 million inhabitants are descended from people who came to the islands thousands of years ago from the continent of Asia. About 500,000 Koreans, 250,000 Chinese, and 90,000 people from the Philippines also live in Japan. About 182,000 people have come to Japan all the way from Brazil. They are the children and grandchildren of Japanese workers who went to Brazil in the 1920s. Another 250,000 people from various parts of the world live in Japan.

Smile! Teenagers fool around with their camera cell phones. ▶

▲ *A rice farm with traditional wooden buildings near the city of Asahikawa.*

Our Country

Japan is a nation of more than 3,000 islands in the Pacific. There are four main islands— Hokkaido, Honshu, Shikoku, and Kyushu. The northern islands are cool and temperate; the southern islands are almost tropical. Japan lies near the coast of the continent of Asia. Its nearest neighbors are China, North Korea, South Korea, and Russia. Mountain ranges stretch from north to south on each of Japan's main islands. Because the islands are narrow, the distance from west coast to east coast is usually less than 200 miles—and often much less. The country's tallest mountain is beautiful Mt. Fuji, whose peak is always covered in snow.

Our Communities

For a small country, Japan has a lot of people. More than nine in ten Japanese live in cities. Japan has two monster-sized cities. The largest is Tokyo, the capital, on the island of Honshu. It has grown so much over the last fifty years that it has spread into several other cities. Together they make up the Tokyo–Yokohama megacity, with more than 30 million people! Japan's other monster city is Kyoto-Osaka-Kobe. In Tokyo, Kyoto, and many of Japan's other cities, most people live in apartments in six-to ten-story buildings. Although Japan is always threatened by earthquakes, Tokyo still has many skyscrapers. In fact, this modern-day city boasts more high-rise buildings than just about any other in Asia! There are some neighborhoods of private homes, built close together to save precious space. Outside the cities, there are villages and small towns where houses have more space around them. But even in the countryside, land is precious. Farmers work fields that climb the sides of mountains. Sometimes the fields reach all the way to the top! Japan is famous for manufacturing cars and trucks; electronics like TVs, DVDs, and wireless telephones; and for computer hardware and software. Many Japanese work in these industries.

A typical Tokyo office ▼

65

What We Eat

Japanese kids like really fresh fish. They like fish so fresh that it hasn't even been cooked! Sushi—nuggets of raw fish served on cooked rice—and sashimi—thin slices of raw fish—are very popular. For centuries, Japanese people have eaten foods from the sea, including all types of fish, clams, crabs and sea urchins—even seaweed. Seaweed is used as a vegetable in soups and stews, as a spice, and to wrap rice for sushi.

Besides fish, the two most basic ingredients in Japanese food are soybeans and rice. Most Japanese meals—even breakfast—include a large serving of rice. Soybeans are fermented to make soy sauce. Natto is fermented soybeans. Lots of kids eat natto with rice for breakfast. Another Japanese favorite is soba, or buckwheat noodles, in a broth. (And it's okay, especially if you're a kid, to slurp your noodles!)

◄ Slurp those noodles!

What We Study

Here are some things Japanese kids learn in school: how to swim and how to ride a unicycle! Besides being fun and healthy, swimming and riding a unicycle are about balance and coordination. What else do Japanese kids study? A full roster of math, science, Japanese, English, art, music, homemaking, and social studies make up the busy school day.

Almost every primary and middle school kid in Japan lives close enough to walk to school. Most get together with classmates and go in groups led by an older kid or a teacher. Most kids wear a hat or helmet in a bright color chosen by their school. (The bright colors are for safety; they make it easier for drivers to see the kids.) At school, kids take off their outside shoes, store them in a locker, and put on a pair of soft "indoor shoes." Every day, students also take time to clean the school.

Many Japanese schoolkids learn on computers. ▼

▲ Little Leaguers line up for a game in Tokyo.

What We Do for Fun

Batter up! **Beisboru** is Japan's favorite sport. (In English it's called baseball.) Kids start playing at an early age. Many Japanese teams have competed in the Little League World Series in the U.S. Baseball is the favorite sport to watch in Japan, too. Some girls and boys also take up gymnastics. Many boys learn **kendo**, an ancient Japanese form of fencing that uses wooden and bamboo swords. Some boys take up **sumo** wrestling. In sumo, wrestlers use their arms to try and force each other out of a very small ring.

Jump rope—group style—is popular at recess. Kids try to get as many people as possible jumping over a long rope at the same time. And of course, as with kids all over the world, computer games are wildly popular in Japan.

No fair! I only have arms to wrestle with!

Holidays and Celebrations

Emperor and empress dolls are set out for Girls' Day. ▲

Boys' Day is celebrated on May 5. (It is also called Children's Day.) Families sail carp-fish–shaped kites above their houses. They fly one carp kite for each boy in the family. Inside the house, boys set up a display of miniature figures with armor and swords that represent ancient Japanese heroes. The house is decorated with iris flowers. The intention behind both holidays is to wish children health, success, and happiness.

▲ *These carp streamers floating in the sky are called koi-no-boli.*

Girls and boys each have their own holiday. Girls' Day is celebrated on March 3. Girls display a set of elegant dolls that represent the emperor and empress and their nobles and servants. The house is also decorated with peach blossoms for good luck. In some families, girls dress up in traditional Japanese silk clothing and invite other girls to visit and celebrate.

Landscape in a Bowl

◀ *This man trims a pine-tree bonsai.*

◀ *An azalea bonsai*

Almost every home in Japan has beautiful small trees and shrubs growing in shallow ceramic containers. The plants look just like full-grown trees in miniature. Some people think these **bonsai** trees are special dwarf varieties of larger plants. They are not. They are regular trees that are constantly trimmed and pruned so they stay small. Raising bonsai trees has been an art in Japan for more than 1,000 years. The custom came from China. At first, only Japan's rulers and nobles raised bonsai. About 300 years ago it became a hobby for everyone. Some bonsai trees can last for hundreds of years. They become part of a family's treasure and are passed from parent to child.

Hi!

Namastee!

Nepal

FAST FACTS

Population:	27,070,666
Area:	54,364 sq. miles
Capital:	Kathmandu
Languages:	Nepali

Our nation's motto is
The Motherland is Worth
More than the Kingdom
of Heaven

Mowgli, buddy,
this place has
everything we need!

68

Who Are We?

Over the centuries, many different people have come to live in Nepal, the "roof of the world." Some came through rugged mountain passes from Tibet and some from the high plains of northern Asia. Most of them settled in Nepal's high mountains. Others came north from the Indian subcontinent. They settled in the valleys and plains areas closer to what is now India. In recent years, adventurers from around the world have come to Nepal to climb its high mountains. Others have come because they were attracted by the way of life of the Nepali people. Nepal is the only officially Hindu country in the world. Most Nepalis are Hindus, but some are Buddhists or Muslims. Others practice a combination of religions.

These two women run a store that sells metal crafts. ▶

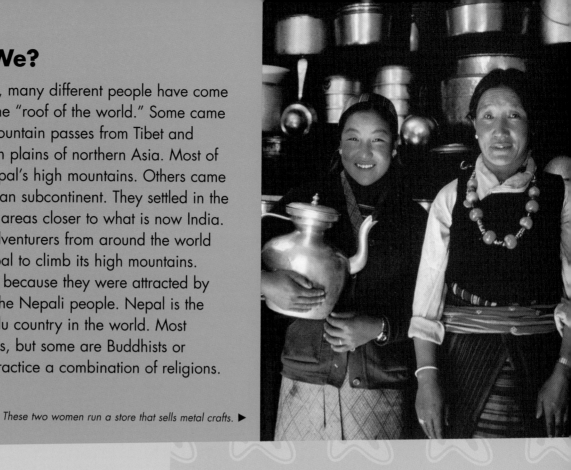

Our Country

Nepal is in southern Asia, landlocked between India and China. The mighty Himalayan mountain range is in the north. Of the world's ten highest mountain peaks, eight are in Nepal. The world's tallest mountain, Everest, is near the border with China. It challenges mountain climbers every year, with its ice-covered slopes, thin air, and jagged peaks. Away from the mountains, Nepal slopes into forested valleys with rushing rivers. Tropical rain forests and plains are found in the south. Near India, the climate is almost tropical.

▼ *Lo Manthang is a walled city in a region of Nepal that borders Tibet. Most of its people are Buddhist.*

Our Communities

▲ *Kathmandu, the capital, is the busiest of Nepal's cities and towns.*

Most people in Nepal live off the land as foresters or farmers, or as crafts workers who use materials gathered from the forests and the earth. Some people work as guides for climbers and explorers. Kathmandu, the capital, is Nepal's largest city. It is a center for the government and for tourists.

69

What We Eat

Nepali kids eat lots of grains. In the warm south, where rice is grown, meals center on a large serving of rice with daal—lentil sauce, spiced vegetables, and a pickled vegetable called achaar. This meal is called daal bhaat. In some parts of Nepal, people eat only two meals a day and both are daal bhaat. In the mountains, people eat other grains and starches: cornmeal, millet flour, potatoes, and buckwheat. Some favorite snacks are rice popped in a hot skillet; rigi kur, which are potato pancakes served with yak butter; and momo, spiced vegetables, chicken, and peppers wrapped in a noodle pouch. A momo looks a bit like a Chinese dumpling.

▲ *Kids buy snacks after school from a street vendor.*

▲ *This group of boys has an outdoor class in good weather.*

What We Study

Until 1951, there were no public schools in Nepal. Education was only for children of the ruling class and the rich. Today there are many educational opportunities, but some children drop out before graduation to work with their families or take care of younger brothers or sisters. More boys than girls go to school. Kids sometimes have to travel long distances to get to school. Some classrooms may have as many as eighty students. The government of Nepal would like more students to finish primary school. It has also started programs to encourage more girls to stay in school.

What We Do for Fun

Cricket and soccer are getting more and more fans—and players—in Nepal. Some boys enjoy learning karate, tae kwan do, and other sports.

Kids everywhere play tag and hide-and-seek and other games that don't need special equipment or a stadium. Mech gumi is a game that's easy to play with a group. Each player puts a stone in a circle. Then a leader takes out one stone. Everyone walks around the outside of the circle until the leader yells "stop." Then each player has to dash to grab a stone. The player who comes up empty is out. The game keeps going until there is only one player left.

Most televisions are in Nepal's cities. Many kids like reading adventure comic books that come from India.

▼ *Many Nepali kids make their own fun—and their own toys.*

Snow Leopards

One of the most beautiful animals of Nepal is the snow leopard. The animal's pale, creamy coat of fur and light gray spots help it blend into the rocky, snow-covered slopes. The leopard's paws are adapted to running across snowfields. The front paws are larger than the back paws, and they have thick tufts of hair between the toes to provide warmth. This spotted cat usually lives in high mountain ranges and is rarely seen by people. Hard as they may be to find, the snow leopards of Nepal are in danger. Even though it is against the law, hunters prize them for their fur, which they sell for coats.

In winter, leopards have trouble finding food and sometimes come down from the high slopes of the Himalayas and kill livestock. This is bad for farmers and bad for the leopards, too, since the farmers then hunt them down in order to protect their farm livestock. To help save the snow leopard, nature groups and the government of Nepal are working with local farmers to build leopard-proof corrals for their animals. The corrals are stone buildings with roofs that keep hungry leopards out!

▲ For several Hindu festivals, Nepalis build and decorate giant carts to carry pictures of an honored god. Sometimes the carts travel from town to town during the festival. It would be considered very bad luck if a cart tipped over.

Come and celebrate, Mowgli. I'll give you a tikka!

Holidays and Celebrations

In Nepal there are many Hindu, Buddhist, and Muslim celebrations. A Hindu celebration kids enjoy is **Tihar**. It is similar to the Indian festival of Diwali. Everyone puts candles and lights all around their house. Kids get to run around outside at night swinging candles or lanterns, and families celebrate with feasts. Tihar takes place in the fall and lasts for five days. The first four days honor different creatures: crows, dogs, cows, and oxen. On the fifth day, girls bless their brothers and cousins. The girls put a **tikka**, a mark made with red powder, on a boy's forehead. Everybody gets new clothes and presents.

This is a very rare sight: two snow leopards at once! They usually roam the mountain slopes alone. ▼

Hi!

Marhaba!

Saudi Arabia

Our country's national anthem is "Long Live our Beloved King."

FAST FACTS

Population: 25,795,938
Area: 756,985 sq. miles
Capital: Riyadh
Languages: Arabic

Yeah, I'm the King of Good Times!

Who Are We?

More than nine tenths of Saudis are Arabs. The rest of the people have roots in the nearby areas of Africa or the Middle East. About 5 million foreigners live in Saudi Arabia as guest workers. They come from Europe, India, the Philippines, the United States, and many other countries. Saudi Arabia is a Muslim country. All Saudis are Muslims.

Picnic on the beach: a Saudi Arabian family takes it easy on the shore of the Red Sea. A mosque with a tall minaret tower is in the background. ▶

Our Country

▼ *Huge deposits of oil were discovered in Saudi Arabia in the 1930s. Before that, Saudi Arabia was not an industrial country. Since then, it has become a modern world power.*

Saudi Arabia is in southwestern Asia, where it takes up much of the Arabian Peninsula. Its neighbors are Iraq, Jordan, Kuwait, Oman, Qatar, the United Arab Emirates, and Yemen. On the west it borders the Red Sea, and on the east it faces the Persian Gulf. Most of Saudi Arabia is made up of sandy desert or dry, pebbled plains. The southeastern part of Saudi Arabia is so deserted that it is called the Empty Quarter! Mountains line up along the west coast. The climate is hot and dry in the desert areas, with nights that can grow very cold. Along the coasts, the weather is hot but humid because sea breezes carry in moisture and some rain. Saudi Arabia has one of the world's biggest supplies of petroleum and natural gas.

Our Communities

Almost everyone in Saudi Arabia lives in cities or large towns. Many cities are near a coast, or grew up around an oasis, an underground source of water in the desert. Some of the cities are ancient, but most have a very modern look. There are shiny skyscrapers, shopping malls, sports stadiums, large universities, hospitals, and parks. Buses, cars, and taxis zoom along wide avenues lined with date palms. In the older areas, narrow streets and alleyways wind around **souks** (marketplaces), and there are many mosques and beautiful old walled homes.

Mecca, a city in western Saudi Arabia, is the birthplace of the Muslim religion. All Muslims are expected to visit there at least once in their lives. At least 2 million Muslims from all over the world visit Mecca each year.

▼ *Riyadh, once an oasis, is now a very large, modern city.*

What We Eat

▲ *In Saudi Arabia you eat only with your right hand.*

Kids in Saudi Arabia pay attention to their table manners—and eat only with the fingers of the right hand. In many homes, families relax on the floor while they eat. Lamb and chicken are typical meats, served with rice. Kabsah is meat or seafood cooked with rice. Dates are eaten at almost every meal. Khobz is a flat bread also served at every meal. Looking for a snack? Try falafel, which are fried chickpeas, or fuul, mashed fava beans mixed with lemon and garlic. Stop at a street stand and get some slices of shwarma—that's lamb cooked on a revolving grill. Thirsty? Kids can choose from many juices and yogurt drinks—or even sip a traditional drink of camel's milk! Saudi Arabia also has plenty of fast-food places that serve ice cream and burgers and fried chicken. One food you will not find is pork. Muslims do not eat pork.

What We Study

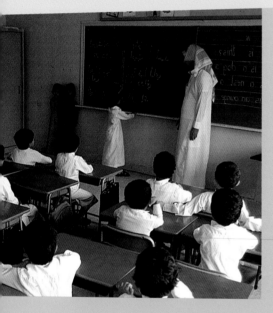

The first thing to know about school in Saudi Arabia is that girls and boys do not go to class together because of their religious beliefs, which teach them that males and females should be separated unless they are close relatives. (In some schools they may be in class together until the third grade.) There are separate schools, or divisions of schools, for girls and boys all the way through university. Girls and boys study the same subjects, although only boys take physical education, and girls take courses in homemaking.

◄ *This all-boy class has an English lesson.*

What We Do for Fun

Girls and boys may play together until girls reach the age of nine or ten. At that age they begin to wear an **abaya**, a long cotton gown that covers them from head to toe in public. At home, when they are alone with family, girls can be more casual. Underneath the abayas, they often wear jeans and trendy clothes. Boys play all sorts of sports: soccer, basketball, track, and swimming are some of the most popular. Girls play sports, too. However, they play where boys and men can't see them, and their coaches are all women. At some sports centers, there are days just for girls and other days just for boys.

Shopping at malls is very popular. Boys and men can wear Western clothing, but women and older girls cover up in dark veils. ▶

Holidays and Celebrations

▲ *A high-spirited camel race is underway!*

Since all Saudi Arabians are Muslim, all their holidays are Muslim. The most important one is **Ramadan**. For one month, anyone who has reached the age of maturity is expected to abstain from eating between sunup and sundown. Non-Muslim visitors or guest workers must be careful not to eat in public during those hours. The day after Ramadan ends is a huge feast called **Eid al-Fitr**. Families and friends gather to celebrate with gifts and wonderful meals.

There is a festival in Saudi Arabia that isn't religious. The Jenadriyah Festival of Arts and Culture celebrates Saudi Arabia's ancient arts, crafts, poetry, music, and sports. A camel race opens the festival. Groups of men come from every region of the country to show off ancient dances. Kids can compete in contests that test what they know about Saudi Arabian history and tradition.

We must be winnin' kid, 'cause I don't see anyone else racing!

Pipelines

Every day in Saudi Arabia at least 8 million barrels of crude oil come gushing out of the ground. Saudi Arabia is also one of the world's largest producers of natural gas. The gas and oil come from wells in the eastern desert or from the sea floor of the Persian Gulf. Once the oil or gas is out of the ground, it has to be moved. Some of it goes directly to ports on the Persian Gulf or all the way across the desert to ports on the Red Sea. From these ports, the oil or natural gas can be put on tanker ships that haul it to Europe, Far Eastern Asia, and the United States. Sometimes oil is sent to refineries. There it can be broken down into products such as gasoline or heating oil. Then it is shipped onward.

The most efficient and fastest way to move that much oil and gas is to send it through a pipeline. A pipeline is a long, connected series of wide metal pipes. Pumps spaced out along the line help keep the oil or gas moving. Saudi Arabia has more than 10,000 miles of pipeline. The Petroline crosses Saudi Arabia from east to west. It can carry 5 million barrels of oil a day. Imagine the work it must have taken to lay that pipe across hundreds of miles of baking Saudi Arabian desert!

When the oil reaches the end of the pipeline, it is pumped into large tanks that hold it until it is loaded onto tankers or piped into refinery towers that break it down into products like gasoline or heating oil.

One way to cross the desert by car is to follow the pipeline. Keep it in view and you won't get lost. ▼

Hi!

Hello!

Singapore

Come on, Baloo,
let's get going!

Our nation's motto is
Onward Singapore.

FAST FACTS

Population: 4,353,893
Area: 267 sq. miles
Capital: Singapore
Languages: English, Malay,
Tamil, Mandarin

Who Are We?

Three quarters of Singaporeans have a Chinese background. They are descendants of people who arrived, mostly over the last two centuries, as traders, workers, or merchants. About one sixth of Singaporeans have roots in Malaysia. That's not a surprise, because Singapore is an island that is tucked up right against the coast of Malaysia. A bit less than a tenth of Singaporeans trace their families to India. Many Indians were brought to Singapore as workers for the British during colonial times. Great Britain ruled Singapore from 1819 to 1963. The rest of the people—less than a fiftieth of the population—come from all over the world. Singaporeans celebrate many religions, especially Buddhism, Islam, Christianity, Hinduism, and Sikhism.

Two schoolgirls line up for a sports contest. ▶

Our Country

Singapore is a city, an island, and a country all in one. This tiny tropical nation sits in a narrow stretch of water between Malaysia and Indonesia. Many ships traveling between the Indian Ocean and the Pacific Ocean or South China Sea pass through this body of water. Most stop in Singapore. Singapore is one of the busiest ports in the world. It also is home to many international banks, multinational companies, and local factories.

▼ Singapore's skyline gleams at the edge of the waterfront.

▲ People walking to the Kapong Glam Mosque

Our Communities

Singapore is a crowded island. Most people live in apartment buildings instead of houses. The government helps new couples and families buy their first apartment. To help families keep close ties, the government encourages young couples to live in apartments no more than a mile from their parents! Single people usually live at home with their parents until they marry. It seems as if there is always a new apartment building going up somewhere! Most of Singapore is very modern, with shiny glass, steel, and concrete skyscrapers; a high-speed commuter train system; parks; and beautiful waterfront areas. Singapore is also one of the safest places in the world. It is known for its low crime.

What We Eat

Food on the run: Singapore may be the fast-food capital of the world. No matter what kind of food you want, it can be found here. Just look for a hawker stall or a food court. All the people who have come here have brought their own types of cooking. They've also mixed it up a bit. Chinese dishes use Malaysian spices like lemongrass and coconut. This Chinese/Malaysian cooking style is called nonyo. A typical nonyo dish is laksa. That's a spicy hot soup made with coconut milk. Since Singapore is a tropical island, cooks use a lot of fish, seafood, tropical vegetables, and fruits. These ingredients are turned into Indian curries or Malaysian stews with rice. A snack kids can find all over Singapore is poh piah—an eggroll filled with grated carrot and turnip. An easy after-school snack? Try a fruit such as a mangosteen, rambutan, or zirzat.

◀ *Throughout Singapore, there are many outdoor restaurants. This one is along the waterfront.*

What We Study

Everybody studies English in school and at least one other language—Malay, Mandarin, or Tamil. The idea is that everyone in Singapore will have a language in common without forgetting their family language. Lots of people speak **Singlish**, which is a Singaporean slang. It combines English, Malay, Tamil, and Mandarin words. Every kid in Singapore goes to school. Education is very important. Schools have nice buildings and good equipment. (Some schools are so up-to-date that kids "scan in" every day with an ID card that has a computer chip in it.) Learning to use a computer is a big part of school life. Being good at science and math is a big deal. At the end of sixth grade kids take an important exam that decides what kind of school they will move on to next. Only the best students move on to top schools.

▼ *Kids are expected to pay close attention in class.*

▲ *To the next level! Game arcades are located in many Singapore malls.*

What We Do for Fun

There's a lot to do in Singapore. In this warm climate, kids can easily spend time outdoors. Singapore has a beautiful bird park and zoo located just outside the city.

There are beautiful beaches on Sentosa Island, just off the main island of Singapore. Schools offer lots of sports activities, and many kids join club teams, especially for soccer and cricket. Some girls and boys play **Sepak takraw**, a fast-moving sport that began as a Malay game. It's like a combination of kickball, soccer, and volleyball, played with a ball made of rattan wood strips. Many girls take up Chinese, Indian, or Malay dancing.

I just gotta dance when I feel the beat!

And for just about everybody, there's TV, videos, and computer games. Kids here may watch some of the same cartoons that kids in many other parts of the world watch.

Holidays and Celebrations

Grade-school kids in Singapore have their own holiday—October 1. They get the day off and some schools even give them gifts!

With so many religions in Singapore, there are many special holidays and festivals. One of the biggest is **Chun Jie**, Chinese New Year. Since so many people trace their roots to China, it is huge. For the two weeks leading up to the actual New Year's eve there are parades, dragon dances, and fireworks. Families clean their houses and buy new clothes. They post good-luck signs and red banners or lanterns on their homes.

All the buildings in Chinatown are lit up with spotlights and strings of holiday lights. On the big night, families gather to celebrate a feast together. On New Year's Day, parents and relatives give children small red packets. These red envelopes hold small amounts of money to wish children happiness and luck.

▲ *For Chun Jie, many Chinese Singaporeans go to their temple to pray. These people are carrying burning incense sticks as they enter.*

Container Ports

Centuries ago, before Singapore even had a name, it was a hideaway for pirates who attacked vessels making their way between the Pacific and Indian Oceans. Today it's one of the world's busiest ports. Ships still make their way through this narrow passage. Many stop in Singapore to drop off and pick up passengers and freight, to restock supplies, and to take on fuel. Today's ships are not the sailing ships that pirates attacked. They are enormous cruise ships and container ships. Container ships are freighters that are built especially to carry big rectangular metal boxes that hold freight. These containers are stacked by the hundreds on the ships' decks. When they reach their destination they are taken off and loaded directly onto trains or trucks, or even into the holds of jet planes, without having to unload the cargo from the containers. This kind of shipping has speeded up the way cargo is shipped around the world. Singapore has one of the most advanced—and speediest—container ports in the world.

▲ *Giant overhead cranes pick up huge containers from stacks as if they were cardboard boxes.*

Hi!

Annyong!

South Korea

Good show, good show!

FAST FACTS

Population: 48,598,175
Area: 38,023 sq. miles
Capital: Seoul
Languages: Korean

Our country's national anthem is "Aeguka" or "The Song of Love for the Country."

Who Are We?

People have lived in South Korea since the Stone Age. Scientists do not know exactly where the original settlers came from, but the Korean language has some ties to languages of northern Asia and Europe, like Finnish and Mongolian. Today's South Koreans may be descendants of people who made their way into the peninsula from the far north of Asia and Europe. Today, almost everyone in Korea shares these roots. South Korea is near China, Russia, and Japan. Over the centuries, those countries have affected South Korea's history and culture. The United States has had large military bases in South Korea for more than fifty years. The Americans stationed there also have brought some of their culture to South Korea.

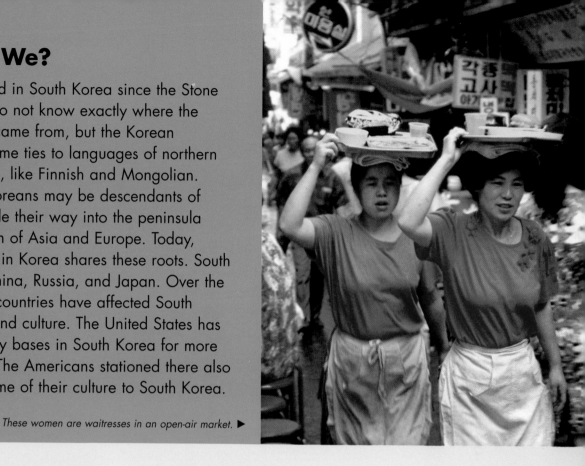

These women are waitresses in an open-air market. ▶

Our Country

South Korea is an East Asian country, taking up the southern half of the Korean peninsula. It borders North Korea, the Sea of Japan, and the Yellow Sea. South Korea has a temperate climate, with short, hot summers and long, cold, dry winters. Spring and fall are short. Along the south and west coasts, the land is flat. It is hilly and mountainous inland.

◀ *The countryside of South Korea is hilly and mountainous. Winter snows in the mountains are frequent—and beautiful.*

Our Communities

At least four fifths of South Korea's people live in cities and suburbs spread around the country. In cities, many people live in large apartment blocks or brick houses built very close together to save space. People in the countryside live in small settlements. In these small towns and villages most people live in houses. Typical country houses were often made of mud bricks, with wood beams and roofs of rice-straw thatch. Some houses of this type are still built today. City or country, house or apartment, the dwelling is probably heated through the floor. For centuries, Koreans heated their houses by running hot air from fireplaces through pipes that ran underneath their floors. Modern houses and apartments are heated with hot water pipes buried in the floors.

▲ *Houses and apartment buildings are side by side in Seoul, South Korea's capital.*

81

What We Eat

South Korean kids will never go hungry as long as there is some kimchi in the house. Kimchi is served at almost every meal. It is spicy, hot, pickled cabbage. It can be a side dish or mixed with other ingredients to make a variety of main dishes. Rice is the most important grain in Korean food, but wheat, millet, and sorghum are also used. A popular rice dish is five-grain rice, which is made from rice, black beans, sweet beans, sorghum, and millet. Beef is the most popular meat served; a typical dish is short ribs in a spicy sauce. Pork, chicken, and seafood are also popular. Many dishes are grilled or stewed. Breakfast is usually the same as any other meal; there are no special breakfast foods. For after-school snacks, kids can stop at a street vendor or small food shop. They might chow down on fried fish on a stick, or gimbap, dried seaweed rolled around rice and a fish or meat stuffing. South Korea also has plenty of burger, taco, and pizza fast-food places.

Hot, hot, hot! Kimchi is a pickled cabbage! ▲
No meals without kimchi.

▲ These boys go to a Catholic school in the capital.

What We Study

Most kids can walk to a neighborhood school in Korea. The first thing they do when they get to school is change shoes. They put their outdoor shoes and coat in a cubby and slip into soft indoor shoes. Kids in school are very polite and bow to their teachers. They study reading and writing, art and music, science, social studies, and math. They may do math problems on a computer, but they also learn how to turn their hands into a calculator. They use **Chisanbop**, a way of doing arithmetic very quickly. Each of the four fingers on the left hand has a value of ten, while the left thumb has a value of fifty. Each of the four fingers on the right hand has a value of one, while the right thumb has a value of five.

What We Do for Fun

South Korean kids like a lot of sports. Just about everybody plays soccer in the school yard. Many kids play on teams, too. Tae Kwan Do is a fighting sport that began in Korea. Lots of kids take it up and compete in tournaments. More and more girls and boys are trying gymnastics, especially since Korean gymnasts won medals at the 2004 Olympics. Little League baseball is hot in Korea, too. Many kids are in-line skaters and skateboarders. Most water sports and winter sports are available in Korea. Korean kids are also music minded. Many study piano or violin or learn traditional Korean dancing and singing. And at the end of the day, using the computer or watching TV is a great way to relax.

▼ Professional soccer is tops for entertainment in South Korea, especially after South Korea hosted the World Cup in 2002.

Holidays and Celebrations

Chusok is Korea's Thanksgiving holiday. It usually takes place in late summer or early fall. It is when everybody goes home to celebrate. Sometimes it seems like the whole country is on the move! People usually gather with the father's family and relations. In many families this is the time to dress up in **hanbok**. These are short jackets worn over long full skirts for women and girls, and short jackets worn over draped pants for men and boys. The family spends days getting ready, including buying the freshest of foods to cook for the big meal. Chusok is a festival of thanks for a good harvest, so dishes are prepared from the fall harvest. **Songphyun**, a rice cake made with sticky ground rice and stuffed with beans, sesame, dates, or chestnuts, is a treat everybody enjoys for chusok.

These performers are in a festival that features masked dancers in traditional costumes, called bong-sa. ▶

Water Deer

▲ *Look at those fangs!*

Take a look at the water deer, which graze at the mouths of South Korea's rivers. These pint-size deer have short front legs, fluffy coats, and short, rounded ears. The males are about two feet tall, and the females are shorter. Adorable, but check out their fangs! Male water deer have two large fangs, which they use to fight off other male deer when they intrude into their territory. Water deer are also unusual because neither the male nor the female has antlers. They can hide among tall reeds and grasses along riverbanks and in marshes. Their sharp hearing alerts them to danger, and they can make a fast getaway.

Sometimes they flatten themselves against the ground to hide from predators. The deer graze on tall grasses and reeds. In winter, when the grasses die, they eat plant shoots and berries. In some places, when their food is scarce they may get into farmers' fields and harm young crops.

You there! Look me in the eyes when I'm speaking to you.

Fluffy Korean water deer have no antlers. ▶

Hi!

Sawadee!

Thailand

Our country's national anthem is "National Hymn."

I just dig that swinging music!

Who Are We?

It's a mystery: three quarters of the Thai population is descended from people who have been here for several thousand years, but scientists do not agree about where they came from. They may have come from northern Asia or from what is now India. Or perhaps they came north from what is now Malaysia. One eighth of Thailand's people have Chinese roots. The rest come from Asia, Europe, Australia, and the United States. Most Thais are Buddhists. About four in one hundred Thais are Muslim, and most of them live in the southern part of the country near the border with Malaysia.

Beach day! Thailand has many beautiful beaches ▶

▲ *Flower farming on the slopes of the Doi Tung Mountains*

Our Country

Thailand is a tropical nation in southeast Asia. The northern part of Thailand is tucked in between Myanmar, Laos, and Cambodia. The southern part is a peninsula that reaches down between the Andaman Sea and the Gulf of Thailand. It connects to Malaysia on its southern border. In late spring, summer, and fall, the weather is hot and rainy. In winter and early spring, the weather is dry and a bit cooler, especially in the northern part of the country. Because of its closeness to the sea, in the southern peninsula the weather is always hot and the air humid.

Our Communities

Thailand's cities and towns are a combination of supermodern and traditional. There are mountain settlements in the north that are so far from roads they see very few visitors. Bangkok, the country's capital, is huge, with skyscrapers, a high-speed elevated train, and lots of industry and traffic. It also has ancient palaces, Buddhist temples, canals with small boats, and houses in traditional Thai styles.

About half the people in Thailand make their living by farming. Many have small farms where they grow rice or fruits and vegetables and keep some animals. Shrimp farming—where farmers raise large amounts of shrimp in ponds instead of going to the sea to catch them—has become a big business. (However, mangrove trees get cut down to make way for the farms, which often results in flooding and other problems.) Thailand is also known for giant farms that raise chickens, ducks, or pigs by the millions.

Thailand has beautiful beaches and hill towns that attract many visitors, and a lot of Thais work in the tourist business. There are also factories that produce goods such as computers, electronics, clothing, and jewelry. Thai silk is known around the world.

In Bangkok people come from very far away to sell their farm products in the market ▶

85

What We Eat

Thai food mixes many flavors—spicy, sweet, and tangy. The base of most meals is sticky rice with small side dishes of fruits, vegetables, seafood or meats, and sauces.

Thai cooks use hot chilies, coconut, coconut milk, peanuts, garlic, basil, tomatoes, and nam pla, a salty sauce made from fermented fish, to add flavor. What's the easiest way to eat a Thai meal of rice and side dishes? Take some sticky rice, make a little ball with it, hold it in your right hand, dip it into a side dish, and then pop it into your mouth! (Or, do what some Thai kids do and use a fork.) Thailand is big on fast food. Almost everywhere, street stands and even boats along rivers and canals sell quick-cooked treats. A popular snack is miang kam, made by wrapping cooked bits of shrimp or meat, coconut, spices, and a hot sauce in a vegetable leaf. For dessert it's hard to beat sangkaya, a pudding made of coconut cream baked in a small round squash. Thai cities and towns are also full of restaurants and fast-food places that serve food from around the world.

◀ *Delicious! Thai food is some of the most refined in the world*

What We Study

Kids in Thailand wear a uniform chosen by their school. It's usually a light-colored shirt and shorts or a skirt. Grade-school kids in Thailand have to keep their hair neat and short—or the teacher might trim it! Children in Thailand are expected to go to school for twelve years. Schools range from one-story wooden buildings with each room opening right onto the playground, to air-conditioned high-tech buildings wired for computers. Kids study reading, writing, math, science, social studies, physical education, art, and music. They may also learn skills like farming and homemaking. More and more schools have computers.

▲ *The high ceilings and big windows of this classroom help cool it in the hot climate.*

I'm ready to box if we run into Shere Khan!

What We Do for Fun

Soccer, table tennis, and badminton are the favorite sports in Thailand. Basketball, volleyball, biking, and swimming are pretty popular, too. Some kids enjoy traditional sports like Thai boxing, which combines kicks and punches. Kite flying is a pastime and a game. Kite flyers move their kites around in the sky to capture or knock down other kites. For city kids, spending time in a mall, watching TV, or listening to music are typical ways to have fun, too. For kids all over Thailand, family time is also important.

◀ *Playing basketball in Chang Mai*

Holidays and Celebrations

Songkran, in the spring, is Thailand's New Year. Families get ready with a good spring cleaning. The festival includes visits to Buddhist temples, giving gifts at the temple, and honoring older relatives. And everyone gets wet! By tradition, people would sprinkle each other with a little scented water to wash away the old year. Today, splashing with water has become a big deal. People chase each other with buckets of water! (Most people think it's lucky to get soaked.)

Loi Krathong is Thailand's thanksgiving festival. When the rainy season ends, Thais give thanks for rains that will give them healthy crops. On the night of the first full moon in November, Thais put small floats in the water. The floats are made from banana leaves folded into the shape of lotus flowers. The "flowers" hold candles and sometimes coins for good luck.

▲ *During the Thai New Year, there is the festival of Songkran. It consists of watering your friends and neighbors.*

Disappearing Elephants

It's hard to believe that such a large animal could vanish, but Asian elephants are in danger. One hundred years ago there were more than 100,000 of them. Many were wild and roamed the large forests of Thailand. Others were captured and tamed. They were used in temples and to transport people and goods. Elephants have also worked in logging and other industries.

Today, both the wild elephant and the working elephant are dying out. There are no more than 2,000 wild elephants in Thailand, and no more than 2,000 tame ones. Much of the forest where elephants once roamed has been cut down for farms and other developments. The elephants have a hard time finding food, and some have starved.

Farmers have also killed some elephants because they trampled the farmers' fields while looking for food. Most of Thailand's tame elephants are out of work. Tractors and trucks now do their jobs. Many working elephants have been abandoned. The Thai government is trying to protect some of the elephants' territory and to help care for sick and aging tame elephants. One plan for helping out-of-work elephants is to turn them into artists! Some elephants like holding a paintbrush with their trunk and painting on canvas. There are now five "art academies" for elephants in Thailand. Money to care for the "artists" and their handlers comes from the sale of elephant art.

▼ *Time for a cool down! Handlers give their working elephants a bath.*

Turkey

Hi!

Merhaba!

Whoa there, little buddy. Let's calm down!

FAST FACTS

Population:	68,893,918
Area:	301,383 sq. miles
Capital:	Ankara
Languages:	Turkish

Our nation's motto is Peace at Home, Peace in the World.

Who Are We?

Over the centuries, many ethnic groups settled in Turkey: Romans, Greeks, Persians, Mongols, Egyptians, Russians, and more. Each group left its mark on the country. The descendants of all these people call themselves Turks, and they make up four fifths of the population of Turkey. The other fifth is a separate ethnic group, the Kurds. For more than 1,000 years, from the 300s to the 1400s, what we now call Turkey was the center of the Byzantine empire. In 1453 the Ottomans conquered Istanbul. Most of Turkey, which was called Anatolia, had already been conquered by the Ottomans, and Anatolia had become a second motherland to Muslim Turks.

Roses are big business in the Region of Roses in southwestern Turkey. The petals are used to make perfume, rose oil, and rose water. ▶

Our Country

▲ *Bodrum is a very old port city on the Aegean Sea.*

Turkey lies where southern Europe and southern Asia meet, in a place called Anatolia. It is bordered on the north by the Black Sea, and on the south and west by the Mediterranean and Aegean Seas. Turkey's Bosporus is an important strait between the Black Sea and the Sea of Marmara, as it connects the Black Sea with the Mediterranean Sea. Turkey has many mountains, with a high plateau in the center. Its neighbors on the west are Greece and Bulgaria. On the east, Turkey borders Georgia, Armenia, and Iran. Its southern neighbors are Iraq and Syria. The country experiences all four seasons, with hot, dry summers and mild, wet winters.

Our Communities

Town of two continents: Istanbul, the largest city in Turkey, stretches across both sides of the Bosporus, which flows along the border between Europe and Asia. So some people of Istanbul live in Europe, and the rest live in Asia! Three fourths of all Turks live in cities or large towns. Most cities have an older section with houses surrounded by neighborhoods full of apartment blocks.

In country villages and small towns most people are farmers or herders. The kind of house someone has depends on what part of the country they live in. Near the Black Sea, many houses are built from wood. In central Turkey, houses are made from stone. Along the Mediterranean, houses are often painted in pastel colors. Most small Turkish towns are built around a small market square, with a mosque, a café, and a school.

These sunny apartments are in the vacation town of Alanya. ▶

What We Eat

Did you know that there are at least 100 different ways to cook eggplant in Turkey? A good Turkish cook knows a lot of those methods, and plenty of ways to cook other veggies, too. It comes in handy for making mezes. These are little appetizers. A dinner in Turkey might start with several meze dishes. Some cooks show off by cooking the same vegetable many different ways! Turkey has a huge range of fruits and vegetables, and they are part of every meal. A popular way to cook meat—usually lamb or chicken—is to grill chunks of it on skewers. These are called kebabs. Dolmas are stuffed vegetables. There are probably as many ways to stuff vegetables as there are ways to cook eggplant! Turkey is known for its sweet desserts. Baklava is a layered pastry coated in honey. Turkish Delight is a candy made with sugar and rose water. Helva is a sweet made from sesame seeds, sugar, and oil.

◄ *Thin rounds of Turkish bread are baked over an open fire.*

What We Study

Most kids in Turkey get to know their teachers really well, as they may have the same one for the first through fifth grade. Students must attend school for at least eight years, beginning at the age of six or seven. After that, they can choose whether to attend high school. Many kids do continue their education, which is important in Turkey. Students who complete high school and go on to college get a good education.

Look out below! A mountain biker grabs some air. ►

◄ *Schoolgirls in uniform do a little shopping after class.*

What We Do for Fun

What would you like to do for fun? Turkey is a big country with a varied climate. Many sports are available; soccer is the most popular. Turkey competes internationally in soccer, and many kids dream of becoming soccer stars. The national women's volleyball teams are successful in international competitions so some girls are taking up the sport. Other popular sports are basketball, handball, and running. Wrestling is considered an ancient sport of Turkey. Backgammon is also a popular game.

Holidays and Celebrations

▲ *Sufism is a type of Islam practiced by a small number of Turks. Whirling dervishes are Sufis who believe that they can get closer to God with dances that match the natural patterns of the world and the universe. Atoms spin, the earth spins, galaxies revolve—and so do whirling dervishes!*

Kids take over! April 23 is National Sovereignty and Children's Day. Schoolkids prepare for weeks for special athletic and musical performances held in stadiums around the country. Some kids are chosen to run the government for the day! Kids replace government officials and get to issue rules about the environment and education. Even the President and Prime Minister give up their roles to kids. In Turkey's parliament, kids debate possible laws about education, children's rights, and health. This celebration has been such a success that the United Nations adopted the idea and declared April 23 International Children's Day around the world.

Stay here and every day can be Children's Day!

Pamukkale

Are they cotton castles? From a distance, the hot springs of Pamukkale look that way. The water in these springs is full of a mineral called calcium carbonate. As the water overflows the natural basin of the springs, the minerals separate out. Over many centuries frozen fountains of stone have built up. Gradually, the mineral deposits have formed amazing shapes. People think the stone looks like cotton because it is bright white, and from a distance the shapes look like delicate drapes of fabric.

The mineral deposits have also surrounded the springs and created shallow terraced pools. Visitors have been amazed at the beauty and oddity of Pamukkale for years. Over time, however, the sheer numbers of people visiting Pamukkale have caused damage to the stone by climbing on it and by wading in the terraced pools. The government of Turkey is putting plans in place to protect this natural wonder.

▼ *These terraced pools of water have formed naturally, over many centuries.*

Let's explore
Oceania!

Oceania, the smallest continent in the world, is a continent of islands. It includes Australia, Papua New Guinea, New Zealand, Fiji, and thousands of other islands in the South Pacific Ocean. The size of the islands ranges from enormous Australia, the world's largest island, to tiny coral islands that have no name.

Cityscape and Lake Wakatipu, Queenstown, New Zealand ▶

The People

You might meet an Australian girl who lives on a cattle station in a rural area called the outback. With no school nearby, she is enrolled in the School of the Air. She talks to her teacher by two-way radio. You could spend time at the beach with a bunch of Aussie kids who are learning to be surf lifesavers. Or you might catch up with a young Fijian fan of his national rugby team. His ancestors settled the islands by outrigger canoe. You could hang out with a Fijian girl whose great, great grandparents came there from India in the early 1900s to work on a sugar plantation.

People first came to Australia from Asia more than 40,000 years ago. Those with roots in Southeast Asia settled the smaller islands by the 1500s, while Europeans came to the continent over the last 300 years.

◀ *Two female lifeguards holding paddleboards*

The Land

▲ *Volcanoes National Park; lava flowing into Pacific Ocean, Hawaii, U.S.A.*

The islands of Oceania are very diverse. The huge island of Australia was once part of Antarctica. Many ages ago, it broke off and drifted north. Volcanoes erupting from the ocean floor formed a number of islands. Still others were formed by coral reefs that gradually grew above the surface of the sea.

The Animals

Oceania has unique animal life. Australia alone has many kinds of mammals found nowhere else, including kangaroos and the platypus, to name two! New Zealand, on the other hand, has only one native mammal: the bat. All the other mammals in New Zealand either floated or flew there! The islands of Oceania are also known for the coral reefs that lie in the waters off their shores. Australia's Great Barrier Reef is the largest reef in the world. All Oceania's reefs, large or small, are home to a huge, colorful range of fish and other animal life.

Two koalas from Australia ▶

The Environment

Reefs protect islands from storm surges and heavy seas. They are also a great source of fish and shellfish. As populations on some islands have grown, however, the reefs have been overfished. Careless tourists diving on the reefs have also caused damage to the delicate coral. Water pollution running off the land also harms coral reefs. Protecting these ocean treasures has become more and more of a challenge.

Coral reefs are delicate structures that support many fish and shellfish. They also protect islands from storm surges. However, the reefs have been overfished and damaged by too much human diving and water pollution. Protecting these ocean treasures has become an important challenge.

*Tuamotu Atol,
coral reef, Tahiti* ▼

Hi!

G'Day!

Australia

I love to travel the entire length of the kingdom!

FAST FACTS

Population: 19,913,144
Area: 2,967,908 sq. miles
Capital: Canberra
Languages: English

Our country's national anthem is "Advance Australia Fair."

Who Are We?

People have been coming to Australia for at least 40,000 years. The first people in Australia, the Aborigines, probably came from Southeast Asia. Another group, the Torres Strait Islanders, lived on a few islands off the northern coast. These two groups had Australia to themselves until Europeans began exploring it in the 1600s. Since then, Australia has been a country of newcomers. The first people came from England, Scotland, Wales, and Ireland. In the twentieth century, people from all over the world began moving to Australia. Australia is still a nation that attracts immigrants. Almost one in four Australians was born somewhere else!

This schoolboy will go out for recess—he has his hat! ▶

▲ *The Sydney Opera House is one of the most recognizable buildings in the world.*

Our Country

Australian kids know their country is nicknamed "Down Under" because it is down under the equator. Australia is the sixth-largest country in the world. It is the only country that takes up a whole island continent. It also includes another big island called Tasmania.

Tasmania is one of Australia's eight states and territories. Australia sits between the Indian and Pacific Oceans. The northeastern coast of Australia has a wet, tropical climate, with some rain forests, and the southern coast has a mild, temperate climate. A mountain range crosses Australia from north to south just inside the eastern coast. Some of the peaks are snow-covered. The mountains and the southern coast have four seasons. Most of the rest of Australia is very dry and very hot in summer. As a matter of fact, Australia is the driest country in the world.

Our Communities

Eight out of ten Australians live no more than thirty-one miles from the ocean, in sparkling cities, towns, and suburban areas. That leaves huge areas of Australia very thinly settled. These areas are called the "outback." Huge sheep or cattle ranches, called "stations" in Australia, take up a lot of room in the outback. Kids on these cattle stations may live far from the nearest town. In some desert outback towns, people beat the heat by going underground. In Andamooka, Coober Pedy, and White Cliffs, houses have been dug into the ground. Some are very fancy, and they are always naturally cooler in summer and warmer in winter than aboveground houses.

▼ *The historic district of Williamstown, near the port city of Melbourne, has 150-year-old buildings and its share of modern ones, too.*

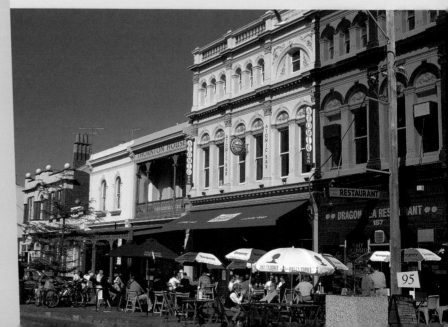

95

What We Eat

Some Australian kids eat bugs—Balmain bugs. (That's a nickname for a kind of crayfish.) From day to day, however, most Australians eat foods with pretty ordinary names—lots of lamb and beef, and seafood near the coasts. Australia grows plenty of tropical fruits like mangoes, bananas, and pineapples. Juicy green-gold Granny Smith apples were first grown in Australia. Australia's many newcomers have also brought the foods of their home countries, so curries from India, Chinese food, Italian pasta, and sausages from Serbia are typical Australian foods. It's also hard to find an Australian home without a barbie—a barbecue—in the backyard and a jar of vegemite in the kitchen. Vegemite is a vegetable spread. Aussies put it on bread and stir it into soups and stews.

Yum! Barbecued sausages ▶

What We Study

Where's your hat? Kids in Australia can't go outside for recess in the hot months without hats. The hats protect them from Australia's strong sun. The school year starts in late January or early February, which is late summer "Down Under. " (Seasons in the southern hemisphere are reversed from those in the northern hemisphere.)

By seventh grade, Australian kids have begun studying a foreign language. Many pick up languages of other Pacific countries. More kids study Japanese than in any other country except for Japan and Korea. Bahasa Indonesia is another popular language to study.

▼ *These girls are part of a junior lifesaving team.*

▼ *These uniformed schoolgirls from Melbourne reflect Australia's diversity.*

What We Do for Fun

Who knew lifesaving could be a sport? More than 100,000 surf lifesavers patrol Australia's beaches. They man lifeboats that pull people in trouble from rough surf. For fun, and practice, they hold surfboat races. Crews launch boats in the surf, climb in and row backward over pounding waves out to sea and back. The first crew to cover the racecourse and get back to the beach wins!

Australia's sunny weather draws kids outside for lots of sports: cricket, tennis, swimming, surfing, scuba diving, running, hang gliding, horseback riding, you name it. Australia also has its own home-grown sport, "Australian rules" football. It is played on an oval field with a ball shaped a bit like an American football. But it is much faster. Players can kick the ball to make a goal or pass it from one player to another by striking it with a good hard punch!

It's so much fun to find treasures like this!

Holidays and Celebrations

When Christmas comes in December, it's summer in Australia. Kids are just getting out of school for their long summer break. There's no snow or crisp weather. Some Australians miss the kind of Christmas people at the top of the globe celebrate. So they hold a second Christmas in July, when the weather is cold. Time to break out the cocoa and marshmallows!

Kids in the state of Victoria get the first Tuesday in November off from school. As a matter of fact, most of Australia stops in its tracks for a few minutes on that day. The country is not honoring an important day in history. Australians are watching a famous horse race, the Melbourne Cup.

Melbourne race day is full of ceremony and fun. Some women attending the race wear fancy hats. There is a contest for the most unusual and most fashionable hats at the race. ▶

Road Trains

Watch out for these road monsters! Many parts of Australia are not served by freight railroads. Yet goods need to be moved across the vast distances of the country. The solution? Road trains. A road train is a powerful truck cab with as many as seven truck trailers towed behind it—like a train, but without tracks! These huge "trains" thunder across the wide spaces of Australia. They stop in towns and farming settlements or cattle stations to deliver and pick up freight. Sometimes they drop off or pick up entire trailers along the way.

▼ *It takes a powerful engine to pull three carloads of freight!*

Hi!

Bula!

Fiji

FAST FACTS

Population: 880,874
Area: 7,055 sq. miles
Capital: Suva
Languages: English

Our nation's motto is
Fear God and Honor the Queen.

I bet I can beat you
to the next island!

Who Are We?

The first people came to the islands of Fiji about 3,500 years ago, by canoe from other islands in the Pacific. In the 1800s, explorers and traders from Europe, Australia, and the Americas came to Fiji. In 1874, the country became a British colony. The British government encouraged people to come from India to work on sugar plantations in Fiji. When Fiji became an independent nation in 1970, half of its people were descendants of the first islanders, almost half had roots in India, and the rest were from other parts of the world.

▲ This group is having fun with the Fijian tradition of wearing a flower behind the ear.

Our Country

Fiji is in the South Pacific. It is a nation of 322 beautiful, and mostly small, islands. (People live on about 100.) Most of the islands were formed from volcanoes, although a few were formed from coral reefs. A few islands were formed as volcanoes erupted from the sea floor. All the islands are edged with fine sand beaches and clear waters. The larger islands have forests that climb the sides of hills and mountains. Fiji has a tropical climate, with average temperatures around 77°F. It gets very rainy from November to April but does not really have a dry season.

◀ Historically, a traditional Fijian house or bure had a thatched roof, but nowadays most villages have wooden houses with corrugated steel roofs.

Our Communities

About six in ten Fijians live in villages scattered throughout the islands, mainly near the coasts. The rest live in towns and small cities. Villages are either Indian or Fijian islander for the most part. In towns and cities, the two groups more readily mix. Most people in villages work in fishing or farming, on large sugar plantations, or in service industries that help the thousands of visitors who come to Fiji each year. Other industries in Fiji include clothing manufacturing, gold and copper mining, coconut-oil processing, and sugar refining.

The town of Levuka on the small island of Ovalau was Fiji's first capital. ▶

99

What We Eat

The most popular Fijian foods are those that can be raised or caught on the islands. Fijians eat a lot of fish, pork, beef, and chicken. These are cooked with local vegetables, fruits, and plants such as sugar cane, coconut milk, limes, yams, and taro roots and leaves. A meal cooked in a lovo, a Fijian oven-pit in the ground, lined with hot rocks, is a special treat. Food is wrapped in banana leaves and placed on the hot rocks. Then the whole thing is covered with taro or palm leaves. Palusami, a pocket of taro leaves holding coconut cream, onions, and meat, is a dish cooked in a lovo. Rourou, taro leaves stewed in coconut milk, is another Fijian favorite. Because almost half of all Fijians trace their roots to India, curries and other Indian dishes are also popular. In Fiji's larger towns, restaurants serve fast food as well as dishes from other countries.

◀ What a catch! This boy has several varieties of fish.

What We Study

Most kids speak Fijian or Hindustani at home, but they speak English in school, where they also study the Fijian language and culture. English, math, science, and history are all studied as well. Kids also pitch in to keep the school clean and to do other chores around the school yard. In many village schools, lunch is a family thing. Parents often bring lunch to their children and eat with them at school.

Neatness counts! This boy is taking care with his work. ▶

What We Do for Fun

Fiji is a great place for playing outdoors. The weather is warm. Many Fijian towns and villages are on the sea, so kids put in a lot of beach time—swimming, spear fishing, learning to use an outrigger canoe, or surfing.

Fijian kids are rugby fans, and no wonder: Fiji's national rugby team is one of the world's best. Many Indian Fijian kids like to play soccer, too.

Scuba diving is a treat in Fiji's clear waters. The coral reefs that surround the islands are full of the sea's most amazing wildlife.

◀ Fiji's national rugby team gets into the action at the Rugby World Cup in 2003.

There are so many amazing things under the sea!

Holidays and Celebrations

Happy New Year, world! Fiji claims to be the first country on Earth to see in the New Year. Fiji is located on the international date line. This is an imaginary line that runs from the North Pole to the South Pole. Since the earth rotates on its axis every twenty-four hours, the international date line is the first place to reach midnight.

In Fiji's villages, people celebrate important occasions like national holidays, weddings, first birthdays, and anniversaries with **mekes**. These are dance ceremonies that tell a story with movement. Some mekes are centuries old and have been passed down from dancer to dancer. Others are invented to celebrate a new event.

▲ These girls perform a meke.

Traditional Indian dances that tell stories of Indian history and religious events are also performed in Fiji. In some Fijian schools, kids learn both mekes and Indian dances.

Coral

If you swim just a few yards off most Fijian shores and put your face in the water, you will have entered another world! An amazing undersea garden stretches out beneath you. There are coral formations that look like giant brains or antlers. Lilac and orange sea fans cling to the coral and wave in the current. Tiny gem-colored fish dart here and there.

Shrimp crawl over the coral. A large moray eel pokes out from a dark cave formed between two brain-coral heads. Enormous schools of fish dart to and fro. They scatter in an instant if a larger fish—like a shark!—comes into range.

How does this "garden" grow? Very slowly, over centuries. A coral formation is actually a clump of millions of tiny animals living in colonies. As each animal dies, it leaves behind a tiny skeleton made of limestone. Over many centuries, the limestone skeletons build up and become the rocky formations we see in the ocean. A healthy coral formation has a thin covering of live animals on it, so it slowly keeps growing and changing.

Coral reefs are delicate and need protection. Swimmers who brush against coral can kill thousands of tiny animals without even noticing. Pollution can destroy entire coral formations and reefs. The government of Fiji is working to preserve its breathtaking underwater treasures.

◄ An incredible variety of sea life and coral sits underwater, just off the shore of Fiji's beaches.

Mike's Travel Journal in Asia

Can you find Boo in the photos?

Rodeo Days

Every July in Ulaan Baator, Mongolia, the cowboys come to town for the Naadan Festival. Many Mongolians make a living as cowboys, herding camels and horses. While many herding families now use pickups and motorcycles to get around, horsemanship is still important. The Naadan Festival is a time when Mongolians enjoy watching their traditional sports: horse racing, Mongolian wrestling, and archery.

Kickboxing Robots

Robots in Japan were originally designed for use in the manufacturing sector, where they perform many jobs. Japan's robots have since branched out into homes—there are now housecleaning robots, "guard dog" robots, cat robots, and even kickboxing robots! A robot kickboxing tournament is held twice a year in Japan. Robots are out of the competition if they are knocked down and can't get up, or if their batteries fail.

Tokyo, Japan

Ulaan Baator, Mongolia

Take the Toy Train

Darjeeling is a beautiful town perched almost 7,000 feet up on the Indian side of the Himalayan Mountains. What's the most fun way to get there? Why, it's the Darjeeling Himalayan Railroad, nicknamed the Toy Train! It's a small engine train with a few cars, running on narrow tracks just two feet wide. This railroad line is only is only fifty-two miles long. It runs from the lowlands to Darjeeling along curves that cling to the sides of the mountain. The ride is so steep that the train has to zigzag up the mountainside!

Darjeeling, India

Don't Look Down!

Here's a hike that will take your breath away. If you visit Sydney, Australia, you can get a bird's-eye view of the city by climbing to the top of the Sydney Harbor Bridge, 440 feet above the surface of the river below! Hikes to the top of the bridge take place even in windy or rainy weather. Climbers clip themselves to a cable that stretches along the arch of the span—so nobody falls off!

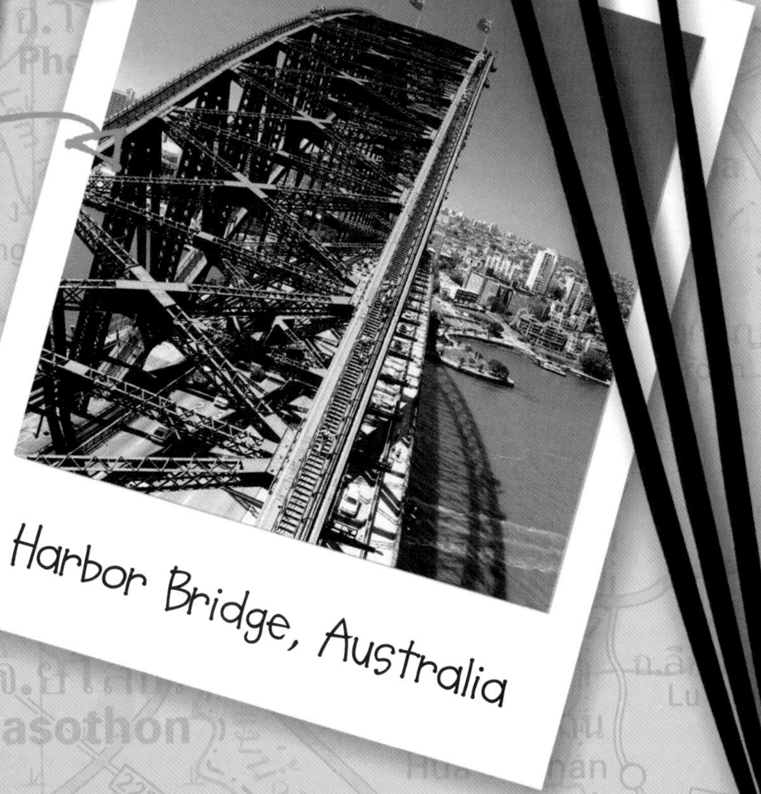

Harbor Bridge, Australia

Mystery Kingdom

The ruins of an ancient Hindu kingdom's capital, including palaces and 60 temples, are hidden deep in the rain forest of Cambodia. The oldest buildings date back 1,200 years. Angkor Wat, the last temple to be completed, is about 850 years old. It has five enormous towers and many courtyards and rooms. In the 1400s, Angkor was conquered by invaders and abandoned. It sat hidden in the rain forest until French explorers came upon it in the 1860s. Pictures carved on the walls tell the history of the kingdom. Today, visitors can see images of daily life, such as people fishing with nets and selling goods in a market. They can also "read" stories about the lives of kings and their battles.

▼ Cambodian riel and South Korean wan notes

Angkor, Cambodia

If You Lived Here

Home, community, food, school, fun, celebrations, places to visit, and more! Kids all around the world have so many common experiences. Here's how kids in Asia and Oceania might enjoy a few more things familiar to many kids around the globe—as well as a peek at some unique events!

Happy Birthday!

An old tradition said that **Australian** kids would get the keys to the house when they turned twenty-one, a sign that they had become adults. Today, most kids have their own house keys at a much younger age, but the tradition carries on. Many kids get twenty-first birthday cards in the shape of a big silver key.

In Japan, it's all about seven-five-three. These are three very important birthday years for Japanese kids. Three is when Japanese kids are supposed to get their first haircuts. At five, boys can wear hakama pants and haori jackets, Japanese clothes of ancient design. Girls can wear their first obi sash around a kimono dress when they reach seven.

> After your haircut you'll be soo beautiful!

What an Event!

> I'll pass that fish, take the lead, and win!

Attend a hermit-crab race at a beach in **Fiji**. The first crab to race off in the right direction and cross the finish line just a few feet away wins!

Check out spider fights in the **Philippines**. "Trainers" catch their three-to four-inch spiders in farm fields and then watch as the spiders "fight" each other as they scurry along a thin rope strung.

The Family Pet

There are almost as many pets in **Australia** as there are people! Birds are the most popular pet, followed by fish, dogs, and cats.

Carp—giant goldfish—are considered extremely valuable pets in **Japan**. Many Japanese apartment buildings do not allow

> Nani, why can't I keep it? You let me have Stitch!

dogs, which are nonetheless still very popular, as are cats.

Dogs are popular pets in **China**—but it can be expensive. Getting a license for a dog in the capital city of Beijing costs $600! Another popular pet in China is the golden pica, a small rodent.

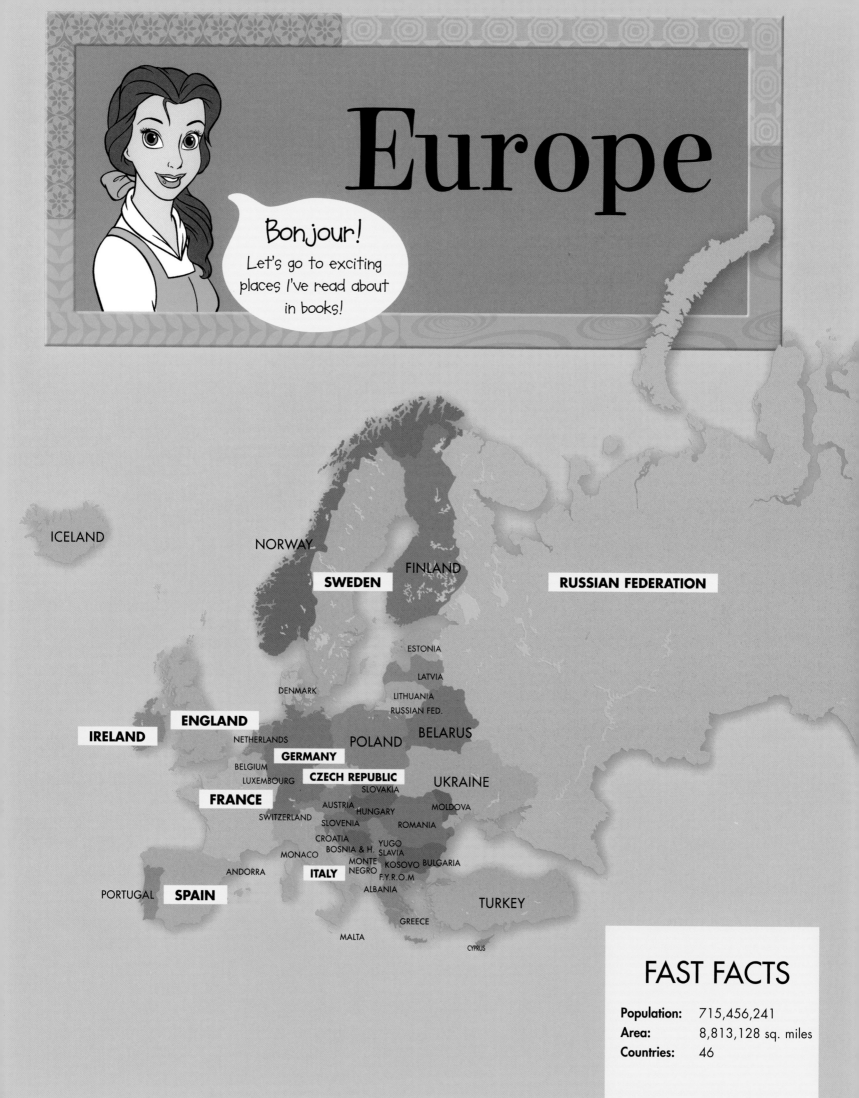

Europe

Bonjour! Let's go to exciting places I've read about in books!

ICELAND

NORWAY

SWEDEN

FINLAND

RUSSIAN FEDERATION

ESTONIA

LATVIA

DENMARK

LITHUANIA

RUSSIAN FED.

ENGLAND

IRELAND

NETHERLANDS

POLAND

BELARUS

GERMANY

BELGIUM

LUXEMBOURG

CZECH REPUBLIC

UKRAINE

SLOVAKIA

FRANCE

AUSTRIA

HUNGARY

MOLDOVA

SWITZERLAND

SLOVENIA

ROMANIA

CROATIA

YUGO SLAVIA

MONACO

BOSNIA & H.

ANDORRA

MONTE NEGRO

KOSOVO BULGARIA

ITALY

F.Y.R.O.M

PORTUGAL

SPAIN

ALBANIA

TURKEY

GREECE

MALTA

CYPRUS

FAST FACTS

Population: 715,456,241
Area: 8,813,128 sq. miles
Countries: 46

Let's take a look at Europe,

the world's second smallest continent with 12 percent of the world's people. (Only Oceania is smaller in land size.) Europe has forty-six countries and 752 million people who collectively speak forty-one major languages. Europe and Asia make up the huge Eurasian landmass.

European Parliament sign, Brussels, Belgium ▶

The People

▲ Monument to the Discovery, Lisbon, Portugal.

Over many centuries, the people of Europe have moved around! Ancient Romans, ancient Greeks, Celts, Vikings, and others spread their cultures, laws, and languages to many parts of Europe. People from North Africa whose Moorish ideas in art and architecture can still be seen in Spain have also influenced Europe. Jewish culture has contributed to the European heritage through its art, literature, and religious thought.

People living in what we today call Europe, developed many interesting innovations and ideas. The ancient Greeks developed democracy for its male citizens. The ancient Romans were great engineers and linked much of Europe with roads and bridges, some of which are still in use today. Several churches that are spread throughout the world today—Roman Catholic, Greek Orthodox, Anglican, Lutheran, Presbyterian, and Methodist—were first developed here. Throughout the centuries, Europe has produced many great thinkers, inventors, artists, musicians, and poets.

After World War II, Europe was divided into east and west because of the Cold War between western European nations and what was then known as the Soviet Union. The fall of the Soviet Union in 1991 changed the map of Europe, as many new nations, such as the Czech Republic, the Ukraine, and Serbia, were created, and old divisions, such as East and West Germany, disappeared. Today, many countries on the continent have joined the European Union, an organization of countries that cooperates on business, the environment, government, and shares a single currency, the Euro. People who live in EU countries now find it easier to move within Europe.

Europe continues to become more and more diverse as people from other continents continue to move there. Kids in schools in London, England collectively speak more than 300 different languages! A street game of football in some neighborhoods of Paris might include kids whose families have roots in Algeria, Senegal, Vietnam, and Martinique. One area of Europe not so diverse is the far north of Sweden, where the kids you'll meet will most likely be Sami. Their families have lived north of the Arctic Circle for centuries, herding reindeer.

The Land

Europe stretches from the Atlantic on its west coast to the Ural Mountains in the middle of Russia. (Only about one third of Russia is in Europe. The rest is considered to be Asian.) Europe has many islands, including the British Isles, Iceland, Greenland, Sardinia, Corsica, Sicily, Malta, and Cyprus. Europe extends north above the cold, icy Arctic circle and goes south to meet the Mediterranean, Ionian, and Aegean Seas, where the weather is very mild.

Europe also has snowcapped mountain ranges, rolling hills, vast plains, an enormous coastline, forests, and many large rivers and lakes.

Many of Europe's people live in large towns and cities, some of which still have very ancient buildings. If you visit Rome, you can see the Coliseum where gladiators fought over 2,000 years ago! Cities such as London, Kiev, and Athens have both old and modern neighborhoods. Other Europeans live on farms, or in villages and towns. Most of Europe's land was settled long ago. There are few truly wild lands left, except in the Arctic regions.

The Environment

Like elsewhere, Europe is faced with the challenge of how to balance the needs of its growing population while safeguarding the environment. Preserving natural habitats for plants and animals, air and water quality, and having enough energy are some of the bigger issues that the governments of many countries have banded together to try to improve.

The Animals

Some amazing animals live in Europe: polar bears, brown bears, ibex mountain goats, white-naped cranes, wildcats, and wolves, to name just a few. Many of Europe's rivers and lakes have large fish such as salmon, pike, and sturgeon. If you're looking for something really big, think about this: scientists have found an ant colony in Europe that is 3,579 miles long! It stretches from the coast of Italy across France to Spain!

▲ White Stork

◄ The Pont du Gard, France

Hi!

Dobry Den!

Czech Republic

FAST FACTS

Population:	10,246,178
Area:	30,450 sq. miles
Capital:	Prague
Languages:	Czech

Our nation's motto is Truth Prevails.

How can I keep this rose alive?

Who Are We?

Most Czechs are Slavs. They are descendants of people who began coming here from Asia about 4,500 years ago. Along the way, they mixed with other people who had settled in the region. The Czech Republic today is also home to Moravians, Poles, Slovaks, Germans, Silesians, Roma (Gypsies), and Hungarians. Many of these people live along the borders of the countries or regions their ancestors were from. Parts of the Czech Republic once belonged to other countries—Poland and Germany, for example. When the borders changed, some of these people stayed put. In some areas, they speak their own language as well as Czech. Most Czechs are Roman Catholics, but many other religions are practiced here as well.

In Prague, young students in Old Town Square. ▶

▲ *The mountains of the high Tatras are divided between Czech Republic and Slovakia.*

Our Communities

Almost three quarters of Czechs live in apartments in cities and big towns. In the country and in smaller towns, many people still live in single-family houses. Whether it's in a house or in an apartment, there are often three generations living together: grandparents, parents, and grandchildren.

Prague, the capital, is considered one of the most beautiful cities in Europe. Even though it went through two major wars in the twentieth century, Prague was never extensively bombed, so it has buildings from many times and styles.

Our Country

The Czech Republic is a landlocked (enclosed or nearly enclosed by land) country in central Europe. The western portion has plains and hills and is surrounded by mountains. The eastern portion has rolling hills and valleys. Germany, Slovakia, Austria, and Poland are its neighbors. What is now the Czech Republic was established in 1993, when the Czech and Slovak people of Czechoslovakia peacefully divided their one country into two—the Czech Republic and Slovakia. For many centuries this land was called Bohemia. Bohemia became a largely independent kingdom in the early 1200s, so the Czech Republic is a new country rich in the history and culture of an ancient one.

Old Town is crowded with people basking in the sun at the café-terrace. ▼

What We Eat

You can't go very long without eating knedlicky, or dumplings, a Czech favorite. Knedlicky are served in some form at most meals. Potato or bread dumplings are served in broth or covered in cream sauce and served with a meat course. You can have a fruit dumpling or kolache for dessert. An apricot or prune filling is put in the center of the dough, baked, and then coated in melted butter and sugar.

Czechs eat a lot of pork, beef, and goose. Typical side dishes—beside dumplings—are potatoes, rice, sauerkraut, or pickles. Wild mushrooms are a popular treat, and some people enjoy picking them in the woods which make up a lot of the Czech countryside. Since the Czech Republic doesn't have a seacoast, seafoods such as sea bass and shrimp are not served very often. But river and lake fish like trout and carp are popular. Man-made lakes, 22,000 of them stocked with carp, are carved into the landscape of the southeast.

◀ *Pivovarsky dum are potato dumplings, stuffed with pork and onions.*

What We Study

Kids start grade school at six and must attend for nine years. After that, they can choose either a four-year high school to prepare for university or a two to four-year school that will prepare them for a job after graduation. Some kids go straight to work-training programs instead of high school.

Grade-school kids attend class every morning, Monday through Friday, and also have afternoon classes once or twice a week. They study Czech, math, social studies, art, music, and crafts. In fourth grade, kids begin studying English. Everybody also takes physical education.

▼ *Interior of the beautiful Strahov Library*

▲ *An ice hockey game with the Czech Olympic team*

What We Do for Fun

Ice hockey and soccer are the pro sports Czechs follow the most. Many kids play soccer and ice hockey as well. So many famous tennis players, including Martina Navratilova and Ivan Lendl, are Czech that many kids are inspired to take up the sport. There are lots of snow-covered mountains in winter, which means winter sports, especially downhill skiing, are very popular.

Some Czech families have a country as well as a city home. Getting away to the country for a weekend to hike, garden, or pick wild berries and mushrooms is popular with Czechs.

Holidays and Celebrations

In the Czech Republic almost every day of the year presents an occasion to celebrate the name of a Christian saint. March 2, for example, is Anezka's day. March 19 is Josef's day. Many Czechs are named for these saints. On January 21, the Anezkas in the Czech Republic get little gifts or cards from friends and family. The Josefs celebrate on March 19, and so on. What if your name isn't on the list of days? Then you just find a name that resembles yours and make that your name day! Many European countries with large Christian populations follow this tradition.

Everyone celebrates New Year's Day. This day not only marks the beginning of a new year, it also marks the birth of the nation. The Czech Republic was founded on January 1, 1993.

Watch me dance at tonight's celebration, Chip!

▲ During the new year, Czechs celebrate the founding of their republic.

Bad Air Days

The Czech Republic has many power plants that burn soft brown coal. Many people also burn this fuel to heat their homes. Burning soft coal gives off sulfur, which causes serious air pollution. The sulfur also mixes with gases and moisture in the air to form acid rain. This rainwater contains chemicals that can harm trees and plants, damage the soil, and gradually eat away the surfaces of buildings and even hard marble and granite statues.

Pollution from factories is bad all year, but when people are also heating their homes with coal it gets even worse. On some winter days, the air pollution in Czech cities and/or in factory areas is so bad that people have to stay indoors. Schoolchildren in some parts of the Czech Republic get gas masks to wear to school on days with very bad pollution.

◄ Shoe factory in Gottwaldov

France

FAST FACTS

Population: 60,424,213
Area: 211,209 sq. miles
Capital: Paris
Language: French

Our nation's motto is Liberty, Equality, Fraternity.

Hi!

bonjour!

It's your turn with Lumiere cherie!

112

Who Are We?

France has always been a land of immigrants. Over many centuries, different ethnic groups have moved here. Celts came to the Atlantic coast. Basques settled in the mountains that cross into Spain. Franks from Eastern Europe came to the northeast. Romans, Greeks, Spaniards, and North Africans built settlements along the Mediterranean, and Vikings came to the north. Over time, all the settlers came to think of themselves as French. In the last 100 years, even more people from around the world have moved to France. Many people from Eastern Europe came to France between 1918 and the 1950s. Beginning in the 1960s, people from former French colonies in Africa, the Caribbean, and Asia moved here. Every group has added to the mix!

Students in Lyon ▶

▲ *Springtime in the center of France, near Billom*

Our Country

Look at the mainland of France on a map and you will see why many French kids call it "the hexagon." It has six sides. It is also the largest country in Western Europe. France's neighbors are Andorra, Belgium, Germany, Luxembourg, Italy, Monaco, Spain, and Switzerland. It also borders the Atlantic Ocean and the Mediterranean Sea. (France also includes the islands of Corsica (in the Mediterranean), Guadeloupe and Martinique (in the Caribbean), and Reunion (in the Indian Ocean). French Guiana, in South America, is also considered part of France.

The mainland of France is varied. Gentle hills and plains roll across the north and west. The Alps, Jura, and Pyrenees mountains bulk up along the south and east. In these high mountain areas, there are mild summers and cold winters. The climate in the north is rainy, with cold winters and mild summers. In the south, near the Mediterranean, the weather is dry, with hot summers and mild winters.

Our Communities

Over the last fifty years, large numbers of people have been moving from the French countryside to the cities and neighboring suburbs. About four in ten French people live in apartments in cities and towns, and six out of ten prefer houses in suburbs of large cities and towns. Farming, however, remains important in France. French farms grow grapes for wine and seeds and grains for oil, and many trees produce fruits like cherries, apples, and pears. About one-quarter of France's workforce labors in cloth making, chemical production, or in car, airplane, or machinery manufacturing. Most French people work in service jobs. They may be teachers, health or office workers, government officials, or employees in restaurants or hotels.

Marseille, founded by the Greeks and located on the Mediterranean border, is the second biggest city in France. ▼

113

What We Eat

Would you eat a cow's stomach? How about snails? Frogs' legs? French cooks seem to be able to make anything into something tasty. France is known for a huge range of dishes! Every region has its specialties. Along the Mediterranean, dishes made with fish, olives, garlic, olive oil, rosemary, and tomatoes rule. In the cold mountain areas, stews, roasted meats, and fondues made with melted cheese and bread are warm and filling. Along the border with Germany, choucroute garnie, a dish of sauerkraut served with potatoes and cured meats, is a classic. Cabbage soup is a dish from central France. Pot-au-feu is a beef and veggie stew from the east. In cities, foods from around the world, especially African, Caribbean, and Asian dishes, are popular.

▲ *Young French baker in his "boulangerie"*

Many families take time to shop each day at small specialty shops that sell items like fruits and vegetables, meats, and baked goods. However, hypermarkets (giant supermarkets) also attract shoppers who pick up food that will last a week or longer. Fast-food restaurants are also becoming popular in France.

▲ *Schoolchildren visiting an exhibition about crocodiles*

What We Study

School is a really big part of kids' lives. The school day starts as early as 8:30 in the morning and goes until 4:30. Some schools have Wednesdays off for sports and other activities—but then kids go to school on Thursdays and on Saturday mornings to make up the time. Kids even get homework to do over summer vacation. School is mandatory from ages 6 to 16. Many kids go on for another two years, and then decide whether or not to take a university entrance exam.

What We Do for Fun

For a lot of kids it's all about bicycles—"bicycle" kicks in soccer or just plain bike riding. Soccer and cycling are two of the most popular sports in France. Kids like to take part—and also to watch—their pro stars and teams. The Tour de France is a world-famous bike race that covers a lot of the country. People in towns along the race route crowd the streets to watch, while the rest of the country watches on TV. In 1998, France hosted the World Cup of soccer—and won!

Skiing and other winter sports are very popular in the French Alps. Kids who live in the Alps learn to ski when they are very young—right after they learn to walk!

Water sports, such as windsurfing and scuba diving, are also popular. Many families also go picnicking and camp out on weekends and holidays.

Fencing is a French traditional sport. ▶

Mont-Saint-Michel

The island of Mont-Saint-Michel, off France's western coast, has an ancient abbey at the top of a rocky hill. The abbey is surrounded by other church buildings, and there's a small village at the base of the hill. Until 1879, during high tide, Mont-Saint-Michel was an island; at low tide it was connected to the mainland by a stretch of sand! In 1879, a raised walkway was built to make crossing from the mainland to Mont-Saint-Michel safe. Before then, people trying to cross the sands could be caught in dangerous quicksand, or they could drown when the tide rushed in. The difference between high and low tide could be as much as forty-two feet!

What a wonderful night for dancing!

▼ *Mont-Saint-Michel is considered a wonder of the western world.*

▲ *Fireworks celebrating Bastille Day over the Arc de Triomphe on the Champs-Elysées*

Holidays and Celebrations

Bastille Day, celebrated on July 14, is a bit like French Independence Day. It honors the day in 1789 when a crowd opened the largest prison in Paris and freed the prisoners, many of whom had been held unjustly by the king's government. This day marked the beginning of the French Revolution. A few years later, France became a republic instead of a kingdom. Bastille Day is celebrated all over France with street fairs, music festivals, fireworks, and parades.

Street fairs are popular in many French towns. Sometimes they are held to celebrate a crop harvest, or to honor a popular saint or an ancient battle. There are music, contests, and games—maybe even a bicycle race or soccer game against another town. And of course, there are booths selling the town's food specialties.

115

Hi!

Guten Tag!

Germany

Free! We're going to be free at last!

FAST FACTS

Population:	82,424,609
Area:	137,828 sq. miles
Capital:	Berlin
Language:	German

Our nation's motto is **Unity and Justice and Freedom.**

Who Are We?

Germany has more people than any other European country except Russia. Nine-tenths of today's Germans are descended from people who probably came to this part of the world from lands near the Baltic Sea. Many other people living in Germany today have Turkish, Greek, Italian, Polish, Russian, Serbo-Croatian, or Spanish roots.

Germany first became a country in 1871, when dozens of small German-speaking areas joined together. People in each of those areas spoke their own versions of German. You can still hear some of the differences in dialect in parts of Germany today.

Young Germans standing by Berlin Wall ▶

Our Country

Germany sits smack in the center of northern Europe. Its neighbors are Denmark, Poland, the Czech Republic, Austria, Switzerland, France, Luxembourg, Belgium, and the Netherlands. On the north, it has coasts on the North and Baltic Seas. Germany is crisscrossed by rivers and has beautiful valleys, broad lowlands, craggy mountains, and thick forests. The powerful Rhine River runs from the mountains of Switzerland through Germany to the North Sea. The country has old-fashioned towns full of buildings hundreds of years old, as well as modern cities gleaming with skyscrapers. Germany is an industrial country, producing much of the world's iron, steel, coal, and chemicals. It also manufactures cars, trucks, buses, ships, heavy machinery, and electronics.

◀ In Cologne, people enjoy outdoor café-tables in Alstadt Place.

Our Communities

Although the country is known for its beautiful farmlands and mountain villages, most Germans live in cities and large towns. In cities, most families reside in apartments; in towns there is a bigger mix of single homes and apartments. Because so many people live close together, Germans take being a good neighbor seriously. Many towns and cities have "quiet hours." These are times during the middle of the day and at night when people are expected not to make noise. Mowing the lawn, playing loud music, using noisy appliances, even washing the car, are forbidden during these hours and on Sundays.

▼ Frankfurt am Main

117

What We Eat

Kids often start the day with a soft-boiled egg, some ham or cheese, a roll with jam, or cereal with milk. At school, they get a snack break at about 10:30. Lunch is the big meal of the day for most Germans. They might start with soup, then have a course of meat, potatoes, or noodles and a vegetable, and finish with dessert—ice cream, fruit, or custard. In late afternoon, many people stop for Kaffee und Kuchen. That's a coffee and cake break. Evening meals are very simple.

Germany is famous for sausages (there are over 100 different kinds!), pickles and preserves, breads, and pastries. Snacks include many kinds of cream and/or jam-filled cakes and doughnuts. Because there are many Turks living in Germany, Turkish restaurants are common. Chinese, Greek, and Italian restaurants are very common as well. And even though Germany has many cafés that specialize in German foods, people also enjoy fast foods like tacos and pizza.

In Turkish restaurants, you can eat delicious kebabs. ▶

What We Study

The school year is long—it runs from August until the end of June. However, the school day is over by lunchtime, usually between 12:00 and 1:00. In some parts of the country kids go to school two or three Saturday mornings a month. In early grades, kids study German, math, art, music, and sports, and take a special class that combines social studies and science.

By fifth or seventh grade, kids move on to another kind of school. Depending on their grades, they can go to a school that prepares them for university, one that prepares them for going to a technical school, or one that gets them ready to go right to work. Some people believe this system is too strict because kids may not know what they are really interested in so early. So new types of high schools include all types of classes.

◀ *Sweet! German families have a tradition for the first day of first grade. Each child gets a large, decorated paper cone called a Schultüte. It holds candies and school supplies.*

I'd be a good swimmer! See what I can do with water?!

What We Do for Fun

Soccer rules here! At least five million people of all ages belong to the German Soccer Federation, playing everything from major league to pickup games in parks. They are also big fans of their pro teams. Germans take part in all types of sports.

Many families belong to sports clubs that promote everything from skiing, hiking, gymnastics, and swimming to ball sports such as soccer, basketball, and tennis. German kids enjoy music of all kinds, and they watch TV and play computer games, too.

▼ *Canoeing along the Danube River, near Kelheim*

Holidays and Celebrations

Happy Anniversary! One of Germany's most famous festivals, Oktoberfest, got its start in 1810. It celebrated the wedding of a king. Today, most people celebrating this autumn festival in Munich probably don't think much about the wedding. They are too busy chowing down great food, listening and dancing to bands, and watching parades.

Many of Germany's other festivals are Christian. Germany has given many Christmas traditions to the world. Decorating an evergreen tree with lights for Christmas began here. German glassmakers are famous for their delicate Christmas-tree ornaments. In some areas, a tree isn't considered complete without a pickle-shaped ornament! It's supposed to bring good luck. On December 6, kids look forward to a visit from St. Nicholas, who brings presents.

◄ *Oktoberfest pole in Münich*

▲ *During the partition, East German artists expressed themselves by painting graffiti on the Wall.*

Berlin Wall

In 1939, the German leaders were men who wanted to conquer Europe. They began World War II. Millions of people died—soldiers as well as ordinary men, women, and children. In 1945, the United States, France, the United Kingdom, and the Soviet Union defeated Germany. The four countries divided Germany. They wanted to make sure it would not attack its neighbors again. They even divided Berlin, the capital. The idea was that Germany would rule itself again when it had created a nonwarlike government. However, in 1949, the Soviet Union declared that East Germany, which it controlled, would be a separate, Communist country. The Communist government kept very tight control of its people. East Germans were rarely allowed to travel to other countries.

Berlin also stayed divided. East Berlin was ruled by East Germany; West Berlin was controlled by West Germany. The city was surrounded by East Germany. While West Berlin became a wealthy city, East Berlin went downhill. The rest of East Germany did not thrive either. Many East Germans went to West Berlin in order to leave East Germany. This did not please the East German government. In 1961, it built a wall to divide East and West Berlin permanently. Guards at the wall shot at anyone trying to cross.

The wall stood for almost 30 years. Then, in 1989, the government of East Germany lost power and the people tore down the wall. The two Germanys became one country again on October 3, 1990.

▼ *Since 1989, the Wall has been a tourist attraction.*

Hi!

Geia!

Greece

FAST FACTS

Population:	10,647,529
Area:	50,942 sq. miles
Capital:	Athens
Language:	Greek

Our nation's motto is
Liberty or Death.

Careful!
You're killing
me!

Who Are We?

Greece is not a very diverse country. Almost all—ninety-eight out of every thousand—Greeks are descended from the ancient people who lived on these lands thousands of years ago. Most of the rest are Turkish, Slavic, Albanian, or from other neighboring countries. Almost all Greeks belong to the Greek Orthodox religion, although there are some other Christians as well as Jews and Muslims.

Sponge diver in the port of Rhodes ▶

Our Country

Greece is the southernmost country in Europe. It curves along the bottom edge of the Balkan Peninsula, facing the Aegean Sea in the east and the Ionian and Mediterranean Seas in the west and south. People live on about 170 of 2,000 Greek islands scattered in the Ionian and Aegean Seas. Some of the other islands are really just big rocks jutting out of the sea. A long spine of mountains curves down the center of Greece. Many islands are also very mountainous. In the mountains and in the north, the climate can be cold and even snowy. But along the coasts it is mild, with hot, dry summers.

▲ *Lycabettus hill and the city of Athens*

Our Communities

Two thirds of Greeks live in cities and large towns. The rest live in small towns and villages. Because the center of Greece is very mountainous, most Greeks live near the seacoasts. Actually, because Greece is narrow, no one lives more than 85 miles from the sea—even people living in the mountains! About one fifth of all Greeks work in farming. Another fifth work in the metal, fabric, food processing, and chemical industries. The rest work in service jobs in offices, hospitals, government, and especially in tourism. Greece is a very popular place to visit because of its beautiful islands, beaches, mountains, and ancient sites.

This is a village on Santorini Island. This island has a huge volcano, which last exploded in 1950. ▶

What We Eat

How about some grilled octopus or fried squid? Those are Greek specialties, as are many types of fish. It's no wonder in a country with such long coastlines and so many islands! Meats such as lamb, goat, and pork are also often on the menu. Greek cooking uses fresh ingredients like lemon, tomatoes, olives, cheese, yogurt, honey, olive oil, and spices such as oregano and garlic.

For breakfast, kids might have a roll with jam, butter, or some honey. Lunch is often a big meal. It could include grilled fish, a salad made with sliced cucumbers, tomatoes, onions, and olives, some salty feta cheese, and some cooked greens. Greece's most famous dessert is baklavah—a layered pastry made with ground nuts, sugar, and honey. But many people have fresh fruit or ice cream for dessert. Late in the afternoon, many families snack on mezedakia—assorted appetizers such as olives, cheese, and small pieces of meat or fish. The evening meal is often light.

◀ Feta salad and green and black cured olives.

What We Study

Kids have to be at least five and a half to start first grade. They must then continue through six years of primary school and at least three years of secondary school. Many kids continue for three more years, choosing either a school that helps them prepare for university or one that teaches them job skills. Kids study Greek, math, art and music, history, and geography. The Greek Orthodox religion is also taught in all public schools. In fourth grade kids also begin studying a foreign language—usually English. The school day lasts from 8:30 A.M. to about 2:30 P.M.

High school celebration ceremony in Thessaloníki ▶

What We Do for Fun

Sports have been very important to the Greeks for many centuries. The first Olympic games were held in Greece in 776 B.C. Greece has also hosted the modern Olympics twice. Olympic sports like wrestling, weight lifting, and track and field are very popular in Greece, as is football, which is the most popular team sport. Because they live so close to the sea, many Greeks like water sports. Kids learn to swim early. Sailing, sea kayaking, windsurfing, and snorkeling are popular.

◀ Greek runner Athanasia Tsoumeléka winning 20 km race at the 2004 Athens Olympic Games

Holidays and Celebrations

Almost every day of the year honors a Christian saint. In fact, most Greeks celebrate their saint's day instead of their birthday. Friends and family give presents, and there may be a party at home. Orthodox Easter is the most important religious celebration in Greece. Families gather in church late on the night before Easter. At midnight, everyone lights candles. There may be fireworks. The next day there will be a big family feast.

In an Olympia Monastery, a father and ▲
his son light Easter candles to celebrate.

There is no brighter candle than me!

Windmill Power

What's old is new again. The first windmills appeared on the Greek islands about 500 years ago. The Greeks used these windmills to draw water from deep wells and to power mills for grinding grain. Visitors to the Greek islands can still see these old-fashioned windmills, some of which are still in use. Visitors can also see some high-tech windmills. Greece plans to make one seventh of its electricity from plentiful energy sources like the wind. The wind may slow down, but it never really runs out! Nonpolluting, it is truly clean-air energy!

Windmill at dusk ▶

123

Hi!

Ciao!

Italy

FAST FACTS

Population:	58,057,477
Area:	116,306 sq. miles
Capital:	Rome
Language:	Italian

Our country's national anthem is "The Song of the Italians."

Who Are We?

Many different ethnic groups have come to live in Italy over the centuries. People from northern Europe, Greece, North Africa, the Middle East, and Spain all arrived over many centuries and settled in different parts of the country. Each group has influenced the history of the country. Today, people from all over the world still come to Italy to live and work. Most people speak Italian. Almost everyone in Italy is Catholic. A small minority of Protestants, Jews, and Muslims also live here.

This young Sicilian woman wears a traditional Sunday scarf. ▶

Our Country

The mainland of Italy is a peninsula shaped like a fancy high-heeled boot. It steps south from Europe into the Mediterranean Sea. Two large islands, Sardinia and Sicily, which are part of Italy, sit in the Mediterranean off the west coast. France, Switzerland, Austria, and Slovenia are Italy's neighbors. Two tiny countries actually lie inside Italy: San Marino on the northeast coast and Vatican City—headquarters of the Catholic Church, a tiny nation in Rome! Italy has two mountain ranges that form a large "T." The Alps range from east to west across the top of the boot, while the Apennines stretch down the center. The river Po flows across a large valley in the north, Italy's best farming area. Most of the rest of the mountainous land is not as good for farming as the Po valley. Italy's industry is also mainly in the north. The country is known for making cars, chemicals, fine fabrics, iron and steel, and food products. Many people also work in service jobs in offices, hospitals, stores, restaurants, and hotels.

◀ *The Tuscany region, near Siena, is beautiful.*

Our Communities

Seven out of ten Italians live in cities and large towns. Most people in cities live in apartments. In smaller towns, people live in single-family houses. Many older Italian houses and apartment buildings are made of stone and have thick walls. Some people live in apartment buildings and houses that are more than 500 years old! However, many Italians live in much newer buildings. Italy is known for its modern, as well as its ancient, architecture. On the southeast coast you can find unusual old-style houses called **trulli**. These are round white houses with cone-shaped roofs made of layered stones. While many people now live in modern housing, these unusual buildings are still home to some.

The late afternoon sun highlights Via della Croce in Roma. ▶

125

What We Eat

Some people claim that an Italian explorer, Marco Polo, brought noodles to Italy after a trip to China in the 1200s. But pasta existed in Italy long before that. Today there are more than one hundred kinds of pasta, in many shapes and sizes: ravioli, lasagna, and fettuccini, to name a few. Pasta is the starch served at most meals in Italy, except in the north. There, rice and polenta—coarse cornmeal—are popular. Italy is famous for good food made from fresh ingredients. Cooks use olive oil, garlic, onions, tomatoes, zucchini, mushrooms, peppers, and eggplant to make amazing dishes with veal,

pork, poultry, and fish. Herbs such as basil, rosemary, and oregano add spice. There are more than 100 types of cheeses made in Italy and many kinds of sausages and cured meats.

Most kids start the day with juice or hot milk mixed with a little coffee, and a roll. Lunch is often the biggest meal of the day. It could include several courses, starting with some raw veggies, cheese, olives, and sliced cold meats. Then comes a soup or salad, followed by a pasta or rice course. After that, there's a meat, fish, or chicken course, served with hot vegetables, and dessert. The evening meal is similar, but often smaller.

◀ *Italy is famous for its pasta dishes.*

What We Study

Which would you prefer? In some schools, kids go to class Monday through Saturday, mornings only. In other schools, classes are Monday through Friday, but the days are longer. Kids study math, Italian, geography and history, social studies, art, music, science, and physical education. Religion classes are optional. In third grade, kids begin to study a foreign language. Kids start grade school when they are six. At fifteen, kids can choose whether they want to keep going to school. (Soon that age will increase to eighteen.) About four out of five go on to high school.

Teenage boy sitting in computer suite in high school ▶

What We Do for Fun

Soccer is so important in Italy that even the smallest village probably has a well-kept soccer field. It may even have lights for playing at night! Kids play. Adults play. Towns and villages have teams that compete with each other. It also seems that everyone follows pro games on TV, radio, and the Internet. Italy's national team has won the World Cup several times.

Italy's Alps have many downhill ski resorts that attract both Italians and visitors from other countries. Italy has produced world-famous downhill racers. The country also has almost 5,000 miles of coastline. That's a lot of beaches and harbors. Water sports and boating are very popular. Movies and music are another important form of entertainment.

Hmmm! The birds' songs are like music!

126

◀ *Skiers ride mountain tramways in Courmayeur, Italian Alps*

▲ Since the Middle Ages, Siena has celebrated the Palio every summer, culminating in two horse races on the Piazza del Campo.

Holidays and Celebrations

Every year, for over 900 years, the ancient city of Siena has held a horse race called the **Palio**. It takes place in the middle of the city square, with each rider representing one of Siena's ancient neighborhoods. Participants in the race wear costumes of the Middle Ages and ride bareback. About 50,000 people crowd into the square to see the spectacle, and people all over Italy watch it on television. The race itself lasts only about a minute and a half, but there are parades honoring the Palio for months in advance, and a pageant and banquets are held in each neighborhood on race day.

All year round, towns in Italy hold food festivals to celebrate their hometown specialties. There are festivals that celebrate everything from sea snails to hazelnuts. Celebrations include street fairs offering dishes made with local ingredients, dances, and silly contests of all sorts, such as hard-boiled-egg eating, running through piles of hazelnuts, grape-stomping, and fish-throwing!

Religious holidays are also important in Italy. Since most people are Christian, holidays such as Christmas and Easter get a lot of attention. The Muslim and Jewish communities observe their own holidays as well.

Letting Off Steam

Mount Etna, an enormous volcano on the island of Sicily, is Italy's most active volcano. While some volcanoes may sleep for thousands of years, Mount Etna keeps busy. Every few months or so, small earthquakes rumble its insides. Often, it lets gas out through vents in its craters, or through gashes that open up on its sides. From time to time, it sends jets of lava and ash streaming into the air. The ash jets may be a mile high. Sometimes Etna explodes with a batch of volcanic "bombs"—spurts of lava that cool into "cannonballs" as they fly through the air. When bits of liquid lava are caught by the wind they make "Pele's hair." The wind stretches the lava into hair-thin, glassy strands. Pele's hair (named for the Hawaiian goddess of volcanoes) can float through the air ten miles from the volcano's vents. Ash thrown from the volcano can land many miles away, too. Sometimes a nearby airport has to close down because the ash from an eruption has covered the runways. Every so often, Mt. Etna has a major eruption. Then, large streams of lava may even threaten buildings on nearby slopes and towns. Volunteers build high barriers of earth to try to turn the lava away. Sometimes it works; the lava piles up on one side of the barrier and cools just enough to keep from going over.

▶ Impressive Mount Etna in Sicily with fiery smoke at its summit

Hi!

Zdravstvuite!

Russia

It's always time for a rousing song!

FAST FACTS

Population:	143,782,338
Area:	6,630,000 sq. miles
Capital:	Moscow
Language:	Russian

Our country's national anthem is "Hymn of the Russian Federation."

Who Are We?

Russia is a diverse country, with people from more than one hundred ethnic groups living inside its borders. Ethnic Russians make up more than four fifths of the population. The Slavs are descended from people who probably began moving into the European part of Russia from western Asia more than 4,000 years ago. Along the way, they also mixed with other people. Many of those living in Russia today have roots in places like eastern Asia, the far north of Europe, and southeastern Europe.

Russian schoolchildren in Moscow ▶

Our Country

Russia stretches through parts of Eastern Europe and all the way across Asia. It is the largest country in the world. It has mountains, seacoasts, deserts, high plains, important rivers, and both the largest nontropical forest and freshwater lake in the world. In the north, it reaches into the ice-covered Arctic. Its neighbors are Azerbaijan, Belarus, China, Estonia, Finland, Georgia, Kazakhstan, North Korea, Latvia, Lithuania, Mongolia, Norway, Poland, and Ukraine.

◀ *Small traditional isba in Goritsy, Russia*

Our Communities

Russia has everything from enormous cities to small country settlements, which can be hundreds of miles from the nearest town. About three quarters of all the people in Russia live in cities, mostly in large apartment buildings. Some of the cities are ancient, while others were built from the ground up less than fifty years ago. Russia has southern seacoast towns with warm weather, beaches, and resorts, as well as northern seaport cities where the ports sometimes close down because of ice in the winter. In the small towns, most houses are made of wood. The styles depend on the climate and location. While most of Russia is in Asia, four fifths of its people live in the European part of the country.

People waiting for the bus in a popular housing quarter in Saint Petersburg ▶

129

What We Eat

Most Russians eat food made with simple ingredients: garlic and onions, cabbage, wheat or rye flour, eggs, potatoes, sour cream, yogurt, curd cheese, pork, beets, carrots, chicken, beef, or fish. From these items, Russian cooks make many kinds of foods, including blini, or small, thin pancakes; shchi, or cabbage soup; golubtsi, or cabbage rolls; borscht, a beet soup served with sour cream; roast chicken; stews of many varieties; and pelmeny, or dumplings filled with minced pork and onions. Cooks in the south of Russia, where the growing season is longer, use lots of fresh vegetables. Many vegetables used in the north are root vegetables, such as beets, carrots, and potatoes. Russia's forests are filled with berries and mushrooms, and many people enjoy picking their own. Russian cities feature fast-food restaurants that serve dishes from other countries. In the Russian places, they have specialties like sausage, or piroshki, little pies filled with meat or potatoes or mushrooms.

◀ *Young girl making pastry for a fruit pie (pirog) in her kitchen*

What We Study

In Russia, kids start first grade when they are six years old. They must go to school for nine years. After that, some students continue on to tenth and eleventh grade while others opt to leave and get a job or attend a technical school. Almost all students who continue through the eleventh grade attend a university for 4-6 years. Science and math are especially important subjects during the school years. Many kids take advanced classes in science and math beginning in grade school. They also study English and other foreign languages. Kids begin to learn chess in first grade because it helps to build sharp minds.

This girl learns computer skills at one of the best schools in Russia ▶

What We Do for Fun

Most of Russia has long winters with lots of ice and snow, so kids find ways to have fun in the cold. They play ice hockey, go sledding, skate, ski, make snowmen, go ice fishing, and even take quick dips in the icy water. Soccer, basketball, gymnastics, and tennis are popular, too. Russia has wonderful circuses and ballet companies. TV and movies and computer games also rule. Big cities have malls and stores with trendy stuff inside, and many Russian kids like cruising them.

◀ *Famous circus artist Andrei Ivakhenko*

Easter eggs are traditionally painted with biblical scenes.

Holidays and Celebrations

They canceled Christmas. For much of the 1900s, Russia had a Communist government that did not encourage religious celebrations. Many of Russia's Christian, Jewish, and Muslim holidays were abandoned, and the Russian government substituted new holidays, such as New Year's. New Year's celebrations included a Christmaslike tree and gift giving, but there was no religious significance attached to any of it. By the end of the 1990s, however, Russia no longer had a Communist government, and many people began to reintroduce religious traditions. Many Russians have roots as Eastern Orthodox Christians. Christmas (celebrated in Russia on January 7) and Easter are once again important celebrations. Muslims and Jews are also free to observe religious holidays like Ramadan and Passover. New Year's remains a very popular holiday.

May this be your happiest year yet, Chip!

Amur Tiger

Was that a tiger bounding through the snow? Aren't tigers tropical?

The Amur forest sits at the far eastern edge of Russia, on the Sea of Japan. It is two forests in one. It is an evergreen forest of the far north. However, warm, moist winds from the sea come ashore in summer. The winds encourage semitropical plants to grow, too. In summer, the forest is a rain forest. It's the perfect habitat for the Amur, or Siberian, tiger. Only about 400 of these tigers exist. During the summer, the thick forest hides them as they hunt and fatten up. In winter, their long fur, an extra layer of fat, and wide paws that work like snowshoes help them to survive. It is illegal to hunt tigers, but poaching remains a problem, especially in winter, when poachers can follow the big cats' paw prints in the snow. Poachers illegally sell the tigers' skins and other parts of their bodies on the black market. Illegal loggers are also cutting down some of the forest, making the tigers' range smaller.

This beautiful Siberian tiger is in danger.

131

Hi!

Hola!

I can see so much from up here, Mom!

Spain

FAST FACTS

Population: 40,280,780
Area: 194,897 sq. miles
Capital: Madrid
Language: Castilian Spanish

Our nation's motto is **Further Beyond!**

Who Are We?

While most Spaniards speak Castilian Spanish, several areas of Spain have their own language and culture. Basques live in the north near France; Catalans live in Catalonia, which stretches down the northeast coast; and Galicians live in the northwest. More than nine in ten Spaniards today are Roman Catholic. However, Muslims from North Africa ruled much of Spain from the 700s until 1502, when all Muslims—were expelled from the country. Today we can still see the effects of Muslim culture in Spain's architecture, art, and customs. Many North Africans still come to live and work in Spain, and the country's warm climate has also attracted many people from northern Europe.

Several generations of a Spanish family pose for a picture. ▶

Our Country

◀ *Andalucia holly farming near Ubeda*

Spain, the second largest country in Western Europe, takes up most of the Iberian Peninsula, which it shares with Portugal. Spain also includes two island chains—the Balearic Islands in the Mediterranean and the Canary Islands in the Atlantic. Spain borders the Atlantic in the west and on the Mediterranean in the east and south. Its neighbors are Andorra, France, Gibraltar, and Portugal. Spain has many high mountains, including the Pyrenees, which make up its border with France. The center of Spain is a high plateau called the **meseta**. Most of the country has a dry, hot climate, but in higher altitudes it can be cold and wet.

Our Communities

More than three quarters of all Spaniards live in cities or towns. In cities, most people live in apartment buildings, while in smaller towns, they live in houses. Spain used to be a country of farmers, but it is now very industrial. Today Spain is known for mining, the processing of metals and chemicals, shipbuilding, and the manufacture of cars, clothing, and shoes. It also hosts about 45 million tourists a year!

Madrid is the capital of Spain. ▼

133

What We Eat

Each area of Spain has its own special dishes. However, most Spanish cooks use the same ingredients: rice, olive oil and olives, garlic, tomatoes, ham, chicken, and seafood. It's the way they prepare the ingredients that is different. Along the southeastern coast, paella, a stew made with rice and vegetables, and seafood, chicken, or rabbit, is typical. Almost everywhere, people enjoy Serrano ham eaten in slices, added to a recipe, or served in a little sandwich for a snack. Looking for dessert? Spain is famous for custards. "Fried milk" is a custard square coated in egg and sugar and browned in oil.

Most Spanish kids eat a light breakfast of milk or juice and a pastry or some bread. They have a midmorning snack at school and then a large lunch at about two o'clock in the afternoon. Lunch is the big meal of the day, when many Spanish families try to eat together. Dinner is a light meal, often served around ten at night, although younger kids eat earlier.

◀ *Ham vendor in Sevilla*

What We Study

Kids start grade school when they are six. They are expected to attend school until they are 16. After that, they may decide to go to high school or they may get a job.

Schools usually start at 9 A.M., then stop for a two-hour lunch break in the early afternoon. Some kids have lunch at school, but many go home to eat with their families. After lunch, kids have another two to three hours of classes. Some schools have started to put all classes into one long session with no lunch break. This way, the school day ends at one or two o'clock, in time for the long lunch at home!

Teacher standing behind two schoolchildren ▶

What We Do for Fun

Soccer and bicycle racing are the two most popular sports in Spain, but the sunny climate is conducive to many other sports, such as swimming, boating, fishing, hiking, and horseback riding. Spain has a homegrown form of handball called **jai alai**, which is an ancient Basque sport. Each player straps a long basket to his hand. The basket is used to catch and bounce a hard ball off a three-walled court. Music and dancing are also big in Spain. Most girls—and many boys—learn traditional Spanish folk dances, such as the **flamenco**, **jota**, or **sevillanas**. Dancing is a part of parties, family celebrations, and especially festivals.

This old teapot still has some dance moves!

134

◀ *These two girls proudly wear flamenco dresses.*

▲ Combatants pelt each other with tomatoes during the annual Tomatina Festival in Bunyol, Spain.

Holidays and Celebrations

Spain has many religious festivals, and Spaniards celebrate Catholic saints' days. Every town and city in Spain has a patron saint, and there is a yearly festival to honor them. Sometimes saints' days are combined with other events. Las Fallas is a festival in Valencia celebrated on St. Joseph Day, March 19, to mark the end of winter. Hundreds of enormous wood and paper sculptures, that poke fun at celebrities and politicians, are set up around the city. Late at night, they are set on fire to celebrate the beginning of spring.

La Tomatina is held on the last Wednesday of August, in Buñol. Thousands of people gather in the main square, where there are also a few tons of ripe tomatoes. From eleven o'clock till one o'clock in the afternoon, everyone picks up the tomatoes and throws them at each other! They wind up covered in tomato pulp and juice. La Tomatina began one day in 1945 when a few friends started throwing tomatoes at each other. Soon, a crowd joined in. It was so much silly fun it became a yearly event. It's one giant mess of a fest!

Bullfighting

Lots of people think of bullfights when they think of Spain. Most towns and cities have a bullring. **Matadors**—bullfighters—take their lives in their hands by going into the ring with an angry bull. The bull has been made angry by **banderilleros**, people whose job it is to jab the bull's back with pointed sticks. The matador teases the bull with a bright swinging cape. The bull charges the cape, which the matador pulls away at the last moment. The matador gets the bull to come closer and closer, until the animal grows too tired to charge. At the end of the bullfight, it is the matador's job to kill the bull with one quick stroke of his sword. Sometimes the bull struggles before it dies, and the crowd boos the matador. In Spain, bullfighting is considered a spectacle and an art. Not everyone approves, however. Many people say it is cruel to kill animals for sport in this way. They want to outlaw bullfights. Bullfights *are* becoming less popular in Spain than they used to be. Some cities have decided to ban them.

Bullfighting is called corrida in Spanish, and it means "race." ▼

Hi!

God Dag!

Sweden

FAST FACTS

Population: 8,986,400
Area: 173,735 sq. miles
Capital: Stockholm
Language: Swedish

Our nation's motto is
For Sweden, with the Times!

Who Are We?

More than four fifths of Swedes are descended from people who came here about 10,000 years ago. They moved north through what are now Germany and Poland. Another very early group were the Sami, nomads who followed reindeer herds in the far north. The Sami came to Sweden between 4,500 and 2,500 years ago, most probably from Asia. Today about 15,000 Sami live in Sweden, mostly north of the Arctic Circle. Other ethnic groups have come to Sweden more recently. One tenth of the people in Sweden are from somewhere else, with many hailing from neighboring Finland. Others come from Yugoslavia, Greece, Turkey, Somalia, and even from as far away as Chile, in South America.

In Sweden, even near the Arctic Circle, you can use your cell phone! ▶

Our Country

Sweden lies on the Scandinavian Peninsula in the far north of Europe. It has a very long coastline, and borders on Norway to the west and Finland on the northeast. Sweden is one of the largest countries in Europe and is also long, running about 1,000 miles from north to south. It is so far north that it would be cold all year long if it weren't for the Gulf Stream, a warm ocean current flowing past the southern part of Scandinavia. The northern part of Sweden, above the Arctic Circle, has a cold and icy climate much of the year. Forests cover much of the country, and there are lakes, rivers, and mountains as well.

◀ *Stockholm, the capital of Sweden, is a town made up of dozens of islands. In winter, the ice freezes all around.*

Our Communities

More than eight in ten Swedes live in cities in the southern and central part of Sweden. Stockholm, the capital, is also Sweden's largest city. Most people in cities live in bright, modern apartments. In areas just outside the cities, there is a mix of apartments and single-family houses. In the country, some people live in old-style farmhouses, often painted red. In the far north, most Sami have given up being nomads. Many live in a modern town in the north called Jokkmokk. When they track their roving reindeer herds across the Arctic they use motorcycles and helicopters.

Paint the town red? It's a tradition in Sweden. ▶

137

What We Eat

If it's Thursday, there must be pea soup for supper, with pancakes for dessert! This tradition is still followed in many families. Restaurants often have pea soup as a special on Thursdays. Swedish food is simple and healthy. Because Sweden has so many lakes and rivers, as well as a very long coastline, fish and seafood make up a large part of what people eat. Salmon, salmon eggs, herring served in many forms, trout, and cod are very popular. Swedes also eat game, such as elk, venison, and reindeer. Fresh lingonberries, red currants, and mushrooms are treats —especially when you pick them yourself. A law in Sweden says everyone is allowed to go into the forest and pick whatever edible plants they want. It's called "Everyman's Right."

◄ *Since the eighteenth century, Swedes have eaten pickled herring and brown bread.*

What We Study

From first through seventh grade, Swedish kids don't get number grades for their work. Parents meet with their kids' teachers to talk about how they are doing. Kids start school at either six or seven and have to stay until they are sixteen. Most kids stay another two to three years after that.

In grade school, kids learn about their country and study the Swedish language, math, and science. In the third grade they begin to learn English. In seventh grade, they add a third language. Everybody also takes child care, shop, computers, music, and art.

Children in class ►

What We Do for Fun

Swedish kids get a lot of exercise all year round. Almost everyone skis. (Swedes claim they invented skis!) In winter they ski downhill or cross-country on marked forest trails or in city parks. Skating and snowmobiling are also fun. For lovers of more extreme sports, there is ice-climbing on frozen waterfalls! In warmer weather many people hike and camp out. "Everyman's Right" also gives Swedes the right to picnic and camp on all open land—as long as they leave their campsites as neat and clean as they found them. Sweden has 90,000 lakes, which attract a lot of canoeists, sailors, and swimmers. Team sports like soccer are also hugely popular with kids. Sweden has produced many famous tennis stars, including Bjorn Borg, which has inspired many kids to take up the sport. And when they have a free moment, kids here like to watch TV shows from around the world and play computer or video games, among other activities.

◄ *Fishing is another pastime in Sweden.*

Holidays and Celebrations

▲ Girl in midsummer dress picking flowers for head crowns

Saint Lucia's Day, on December 13, is one of the most famous Swedish celebrations. The oldest girl in the house dresses up in a long white dress with a wreath of candles in her hair. She and the rest of the kids in the house carry trays of dessert to the adults, and sing Christmas songs.

North of the Arctic Circle, the Sami hold a 400-year-old market festival. Every February they gather in the town of Lokkmokk to trade reindeer skins, objects made from reindeer horns, food, and embroidered crafts. At the end of the fair they hold a reindeer race on a frozen lake. Years and years ago, the Sami came to their fair by reindeer sled or on skis. A few still do for fun, but today most come by truck or snowmobile.

It looks like a maypole—but it's not! It's a midsummer pole. Swedes celebrate Midsummer Day on the third weekend in June, which is close to the longest day of the year. It's a day for picnics and outdoor games and dancing around the pole.

This is the midsummer pole raised in June. ▼

Aurora borealis illuminates the sky above the Northwest territories. ▲

Northern Lights

In Sweden, days are very long in summer—and short in winter. Above the Arctic Circle there are winter days that stay almost completely dark, but that doesn't mean there is no natural light. Like other people who live in the far north, Swedes can enjoy the aurora borealis, also known as the northern lights. The northern lights are an amazing display: dancing waves of colored lights against the dark sky. They occur when bits of energy from storms on the sun reach the Earth's atmosphere. The energy is attracted by the magnetism over the Earth's poles, and when particles bump into gas atoms in the atmosphere, the gases give off light. The light comes in shades of green, red, or purple, depending on the gas and its altitude. It's quite a show!

Very nice, but it is not as bright as Lumiere, no?

139

Hi!

Hello!

United Kingdom

Our country's national anthem
is "God Save the Queen."

This little
number is
majestic, too!

140

Who Are We?

The United Kingdom is very diverse. Over the ages, it has been home to many ethnic groups. The first people probably came from central Europe; then came the Romans, followed by the Saxons and Angles (from whom the name "England" is derived) and then the Vikings came in from the far North. The Normans arrived next, from France. Over the centuries, these people mixed and formed the culture of the United Kingdom. In the second half of the twentieth century, people from all over the world came to live here. Many were from countries once ruled by the United Kingdom, such as: Nigeria, Kenya, South Africa, Tanzania, Pakistan, India, many Caribbean islands, and Hong Kong. Everyone brought their own customs and language. The language and culture of the United Kingdom today are a combination of all these influences.

Scottish teens studying ▶

▲ *Snowdonia National Park, Wales*

Our Communities

Three quarters of the land is used for farming and herding. However, only a small number of people with expensive equipment can manage a big farm these days. So farming areas are thinly settled. Nine out of ten people crowd into cities and suburbs. *Crowd* is the right word, too. The cities and towns take up less than one tenth of the land!

In the 1800s, the United Kingdom was the most industrialized country in the world. Today, only one fourth of the people work in industry. The United Kingdom still produces cars, planes, chemicals, and electronic equipment, but most people are either health, government, or office workers, or have jobs in places like stores, hotels, and restaurants.

Our Country

The United Kingdom is an island nation in the North Atlantic, about twenty-two miles off the coast of France. It is made up of the island of Great Britain, which consists of England, Wales, and Scotland, and also the northern part of the island of Ireland. Smaller islands such as the Isle of Wight, the Scilly Isles, the Hebrides, the Shetlands, and the Orkney Islands are also part of the United Kingdom. In the north and west, mountains and steep hills are cut with deep valleys; the south and southeast have more rolling hills and plains. The United Kingdom should be very cold because it is so far north. However, the Gulf Stream passes by its west coast. This water current brings warmth all the way from the Caribbean, so the United Kingdom has a temperate, often rainy, climate.

Rows of terrace houses in Brighton, East Sussex ▼

What We Eat

Bubble and squeak! Bangers and mash! Bubble and squeak are fried mashed potatoes, cabbage, and other veggies. Bangers and mash are potatoes and sausage. This used to be a meat and potatoes kind of nation, where simple stews and roasts with potatoes, as well as fish, had always been popular. In fact, fish–and–chips may have been the first fast food. In the 1800s, shops began selling take–out orders of fried codfish and fries. Today, fast-food places also serve burgers, Indian snacks, noodles, pizza, and much more.

Immigrants have brought their favorite recipes with them, and food stores sell everything from pastas and taco shells to the makings for Indian, African, and Asian foods. Restaurants and home cooks serve foods from many countries.

The *way* people eat has changed, too. Kids used to eat a breakfast that included eggs, bacon or sausage, cereal, and fruit. Then they would have a large meal at school, and tea—a light supper—late in the afternoon. Now many people have a light breakfast, a light lunch, a cup of tea or milk in the afternoon, and dinner—the largest meal—at night.

Bangers and mash. ▲

What We Study

Kids start school when they are five. In the United Kingdom, the first two years of primary school are often called "infant school." But it's not for babies—there's much to learn! The next four years are spent in junior school. Many schools—but not all—have uniforms. Each school chooses its own.

Kids must stay in school until they are sixteen. Then they can choose whether to go out to work or stay in school for another two years. (About two thirds continue.) In Wales, about 500,000 people speak Welsh, an ancient language. Most schools in Wales teach some classes in Welsh. In Scotland and Northern Ireland, small groups speak another ancient language, Gaelic. Some schools in each area teach courses in the language. Everybody in the United Kingdom studies English, math, art, music, science, and history or social studies.

◀ *Schoolchildren using covered walkway in a college*

What We Do for Fun

Many sports were invented here: soccer, cricket, rugby, tennis, and squash for starters. Other sports, like golf and boxing, may have started somewhere else—but the rules were invented here! It's no wonder that all of these sports, especially soccer, rugby, and cricket, have lots of fans.

Filmmaking got started early here, and today there are a number of studios making world-famous movies. Going to the movies is a popular weekend activity for kids and adults. Watching the telly (television) is also tops—and so is going online.

Going to a leisure complex is fun. ▶

▲ These Scots wear skirts! It's called a kilt. Edinburgh Festival.

Holidays and Celebrations

Each part of the United Kingdom has its own traditions. May Day signals the beginning of summer in England. In the center of many towns, maypoles—some sixty feet high or more—are set up. Dancers weave in and around the pole. Street fairs, with dancers and music, are everywhere. Musical choir festivals are a major tradition in Wales. In Scotland, the summer features Highland games with bagpipes, unusual athletic contests like tossing the caber (a heavy wooden pole), and feasts.

A newer celebration is the Notting Hill Carnival in August. This is a Caribbean-style event, featuring Caribbean foods, costume parades, reggae musicians, and steel-drum bands. It has become the biggest street carnival in Europe.

That maypole is enormous! I must cut it down to size!

Stonehenge

Stonehenge is a 5,000-year-old mystery. Located on a plain in England, Stonehenge is a circle of huge standing stones, ditches, mounds, holes in the ground, and graves. People began this site long before the invention of the wheel, using bones and antlers as tools. They spent about 1,500 years working on Stonehenge. But by the time the Romans arrived in 55 B.C., the circle had been abandoned. No one really knows what the stones were for, but scientists have some ideas. If you stand inside the main circle at dawn on June 21 or 22 (the longest day of the year), face east, and look through two tall stones at a smaller stone outside the ring, you'll see the sun rise directly over the smaller stone. Some scientists also believe that the placement of the other stones and holes allowed ancient people to count off months and seasons. It even allowed them to calculate eclipses of the moon. To many scientists, Stonehenge is an ancient calendar. Of course, not everyone agrees. Some scientists think Stonehenge was an ancient temple, perhaps even the burial place of kings. Whatever Stonehenge once was, it is now a reminder that people lived here long before history was recorded. It also shows what amazing things people could create with only a few basic tools.

▼ In the Salisbury Plain, you can see the huge prehistoric monument of Stonehenge.

143

Mike's Travel Journal in Europe

Can you find Sully in the photos?

Greetings from the Coolest Spot in Sweden!

Every winter guests come to stay at the Ice Hotel in Sweden's far north. The entire building is carved from ice and snow. Sculptures in the lobby, hanging light fixtures, and furniture are all made from ice. Guests sleep in heavy-duty sleeping bags on ice beds covered with fur throws. The only problem is there is no comfy way to make an ice bathroom! (Heated, ordinary bathrooms are located in a separate building.) Every year, the hotel is rebuilt because the ice melts in spring and the hotel slips away!

Ice Hotel, Sweden

Castle Fantasy

Is there a fairy godmother here? You might wonder when you see Neuschwanstein castle in the German Alps. It's the perfect fairy tale castle, and looks as if it might be 600 years old. It has tall round towers and guardhouses and high spires. In spite of its looks, Neuschwanstein isn't that old. King Ludwig of Bavaria built it about 150 years ago. He wanted to build his idea of a great castle.

This Tour Is Worth Its Salt

One of Poland's most famous tourist attractions is the Wieliczk, a salt mine near Cracow. People have been mining rock salt here for more than 900 years. Over all that time they carved out more than 2,000 enormous underground caverns. The miners turned some of the caverns into ballrooms, orchestra halls, and chapels. The halls and tunnels are decorated with sculptures and chandeliers made from rock salt. It's an amazing sight!

Wieliczk, Poland

Bavaria, German

Chugging Through the Chunnel

For many centuries the British Isles were separated from the rest of Europe by the English Channel, the narrow body of water between England and France. In the 1800s, people began dreaming about a tunnel between the two countries. However, work didn't start on the "Chunnel Tunnel" until 1988. It's actually three tunnels 31 miles long dug deep into the seabed. Building the Chunnel was quite a job. Teams of drillers using enormous cutting machines started from opposite sides and raced to meet in the center. The Chunnel opened for business in 1994.

London, England

Meet You at the Snack Bar!

You can take your time walking around the streets of Pompeii, an old Italian city. Poke your head into a bakery and see hundreds of loaves of bread stacked in the oven. Walk past a snack bar. There's nobody inside and although it looks open for business, nobody has lived here for almost 2,000 years! A nearby volcano, Mt. Vesuvius, erupted, and almost overnight buried the city in tons of ash. The ash fell so quickly that the buildings and belongings of the people were preserved just as they were. The city was buried for about 1,700 years, until a farmer digging in a field discovered it. Scientists have spent the years since then uncovering Pompeii.

Euro coins ▼

Pompeii, Italy

Ride 'em, Cowboy!

French cowboys, called gardians, ride the range in the Camargue, in the south of France. The Camargue, a delta of the Rhone River, is full of flat, salty marshes. Wild Camargue ponies roam the area in small herds. The ponies are a small, sturdy, and unusual breed, born with dark, almost black coats that fade almost to white once they are grown. Gardians round up some of the ponies every year and train them to help ride herd on the black bulls also famous in the Camargue.

Camargue, France

If You Lived Here

Home, community, food, school, fun, celebrations, places to visit, and more! Kids all around the world have so many common experiences. Here's how kids in Europe might enjoy a few more things familiar to many kids around the globe—as well as a peek at some unique events!

Happy Birthday!

In Denmark, families fly a flag outside their house or apartment window to show that someone inside is celebrating a birthday.

In most European countries, birthdays are celebrated with a cake decorated with a candle for every year of a kid's life. In some places, an extra candle is added for the birthday kid "to grow on." The tradition of a birthday cake with candles may have started in Germany. Now it is a tradition in many parts of the world.

> Stitch likes a little ice cream to wash down birthday cake.

What an Event!

> AAAHH! Pancakes are for eating not running!

If you can run and flip a pancake at the same time, then you should enter the pancake races held in many towns in **England** on Shrove Tuesday, the day before the beginning of the Christian season of Lent. The idea is to race through the town square to a local church, frying pan in hand. Runners have to flip a pancake three times during the race.

You could enter the annual cart-wheel competition in Dusseldorf, **Germany**. Kids are judged for how fast and how well they can cartwheel.

During the mid-winter festival in **Iceland**, people feast on the kind of foods their Viking ancestors lived on hundreds of years ago: boiled lamb's head, liver pudding, and shark meat that has aged so much it's almost rotten!

The Family Pet

> Smile, Stitch! Let's take your passport photo!

The European Union offers passports for dogs, cats, and ferrets. The passports prove that the animals have had all their shots and checkups and do not have any contagious diseases.

In England one in every two households has at least one pet.

In Italy, your pet would more likely be a cat than a dog.

Latin America

Hola! We can't wait to see Latin America, can you!

MEXICO

CUBA

DOMINICAN REPUBLIC

HAITI

JAMAICA

BELIZE

ST KITTS AND NEVIS

ANTIGUA AND BARBUDA

GUATEMALA   HONDURAS

DOMINICA

EL SALVADOR   NICARAGUA

ST LUCIA

GRENADA

BARBADOS

ST VINCENT AND THE GRENADINES

COSTA RICA

TRINIDAD AND TOBAGO

PANAMA

VENEZUELA

GUYANA

COLOMBIA

SURINAME   FRENCH GUIANA

ECUADOR

BRAZIL

PERU

BOLIVIA

PARAGUAY

URUGUAY

CHILE   ARGENTINA

FAST FACTS

Population: 742,987,237
Area: 7,140,808 sq. miles
Countries: 32

Let's explore Latin America!

> I think Minnie would love a trip to Latin America!

Latin America is not a continent like Europe or Asia. Instead, it is an area that spreads over part of North, and most of South America, and also includes many Caribbean islands. It gets its name from the Europeans who began settling in the area in the 1500s. They came from Spain, France, and Portugal, places where the languages were based on Latin.

▲ Young boys cheering at a soccer match

The People

The story of Latin America is the story of three groups: the Native Americans who were the first people here; the Europeans who began coming in the 1500s; and the Africans who were brought by the Europeans to work as slaves. Over time, many descendants of these groups mixed. Many Latin Americans have roots in all three cultures. Today, Latin Americans make up eight percent of the world's population.

What kind of kids could you meet? You might run into an eleven-year-old Mayan girl in Merida, Mexico. Her father is a guide to the Mayan ruins of Chichen Itza, an ancient rain forest city built long before Europeans set foot in America.

In San Jose, Costa Rica, you could meet a boy who windsurfs on a lake near his city. His ancestors came from Spain about 250 years ago. In the Amazon rain forest, on the border of Brazil and Peru, a brother and sister from a small Native American community catch fish from the river, much like their ancestors have done for thousands of years. In Brasilia, the capital of Brazil, you could run into another brother and sister coming out of

their high-rise apartment on the way to school. Their father is a government official, and they have ancestors whose roots are Native American, German, Portuguese, and African.

▼ Mayan girl near the Castillo pyramid, Mexico

The Land

Latin America covers a lot of territory. It includes the North American country of Mexico; the Central American countries of Guatemala, Costa Rica, Honduras, Nicaragua, El Salvador, and Panama; and most of the countries of South America. (That continent is very long. It angles south past the equator almost to the icy cold continent of Antarctica.) Latin America also includes many Caribbean islands. The geography of Latin America offers up just about everything. The Andes Mountains of South America are especially impressive. They are 5,000 miles long and range down the western side of the continent from the very north to its southern tip. Some peaks are 22,000 feet high! Latin America also has the second longest river in the world, the Amazon. One fifth of the world's fresh water flows along its banks. Then there's the Amazon rain forest, the largest in the world. Latin America also features the driest place on Earth, the Atacama Desert, located on the west coast of Chile.

The Animals

Latin America has huge numbers of domesticated animals: cattle, llamas, sheep, and goats graze highland farms and grassy plains. On the wild side there are thousands of species, some that exist nowhere else, like the capybara, the world's largest rodent, which can weigh up to 100 pounds! Dolphins join other marine life along Latin America's coasts. The plains of Argentina and Brazil are home to the rhea, a flightless bird that looks like a small ostrich. The Amazon rain forest has 2,000 species of fish, 8,000 species of insects, and more than 1,500 species of birds!

The Environment

The rain forests of Latin America are a treasure-house of animals and plants. (Scientists have used plants discovered here in many life-changing medicines.) The trees here provide clean, fresh air for the world. They absorb carbon dioxide gas from the air and give off oxygen in return.

However, much of the Amazon rain forest and the rain forest in Costa Rica have been cleared so farmers and ranchers can raise crops and cattle. In some areas of the Amazon, trees have been cut away to make room for gold mining. Chemicals from the mining operations pollute the air and water. Other parts of the forest have been logged for lumber and paper production. Chemicals from the paper mills also pollute the water. Some species of animals and plants are on the verge of dying out because of pollution or the loss of habitat.

Governments are working hard to stem the losses. Logging and land clearing are now regulated, and people are learning how to make a living in the rain forest without harming it. Nature organizations are also working to ensure new growth where trees have been cut down.

◄ Young girl with alpaca; Peru

Hi!

Hola!

Argentina

FAST FACTS

Population:	39,144,753
Area:	1,068,296 sq. miles
Capital:	Buenos Aires
Languages:	Spanish

Our nation's motto is
In Union and Liberty.

See, Minnie, we can do anything as long as we're together!

Who Are We?

More than four fifths of Argentines have roots in Europe. Most are descendants of Spanish and Italian immigrants. A tiny portion of the population is Native American or mestizo (a Native American and European mix). Most of the rest of the people have roots in other South American countries, or in Japan, Syria, or Lebanon. Spanish is the official language, with Italian a close runner-up. Catholicism is the official religion. About one in fifty Argentines is Protestant. Argentina has about 300,000 Jewish people, which is the largest Jewish population in Latin America. It also has the largest Islamic mosque.

A gaucho, or Argentine cowboy, entertains at a festival. ▶

Our Country

Argentina is the second-largest country in South America. Bolivia and Paraguay border its swampy and wooded northern area. Brazil and Uruguay sit on its northeast side. Argentina's beautiful beaches and its capital, Buenos Aires, are on the eastern coast. The Andes Mountains form a natural wall down the western border with Chile. Stretching across Argentina's middle are the pampas. These flat, grassy plains have very fertile soil. It's also where huge herds of livestock graze. Cool, dry Patagonia is to the south. Here there are stony, flat plateaus, waterfalls, desert, mountains, dense forests, glaciers, and lakes. Argentina's climate is mostly temperate. In the far north it is usually hot and wet, and in the far south it is cold and dry.

◀ *These wide-open pampas in Patagonia stretch toward the Andes Mountains in the distance.*

Our Communities

About nine tenths of all Argentines live in cities and towns. Buenos Aires, with its suburbs, has about thirteen million people. That makes it one of the largest cities in the world. Many Argentines own small businesses or have industry, government, or professional jobs. Most live in apartment buildings or single houses with small yards.

Large companies often own **estancias**, large farms and ranches found in country areas. Some of the largest estancias are so big that there are churches and schools on the property. The cowboys who work on ranching estancias are called **gauchos**. Other people in country areas may live in small towns and have small farms.

▼ *Buenos Aires was designed with wide avenues. This one is the widest street in the world!*

151

What We Eat

Argentina is not an easy place for people who don't like to eat meat. Meat is the centerpiece of most meals. Parrilla is a platter of all sorts of grilled meats—steaks, sausages, and kidneys. Carne Asado—barbecued beef or goat—is another typical dish. Other favorites include locro, a stew made of hominy, beef, onion, tomato, sausage, squash, and potatoes, and milanesa, which is panfried steak or veal. Pasta dishes made with raviolis or noquis (Spanish for "gnocchi") are Italian foods with an Argentine twist. Looking for a snack that's easy to carry? Empanadas are turnover pastries often filled with spicy beef, cheese, or spinach. There are even fruit-filled dessert empanadas. Speaking of dessert, alfajores are cookie sandwiches filled with jam, chocolate, or caramel. Maté is a popular herb tea invented by gauchos. It is served in a gourd with a metal straw.

◀ *Barbecue time! This cook is grilling meat on an open fire for a parrilla.*

What We Study

Most primary school kids in Argentina don't wear uniforms, but they do put white smocks over their clothes to keep their clothes clean. They start kindergarten at age five and can stop their schooling when they are fifteen, or they can choose to go on to either a three-year high school or a vocational school. Many kids go to school from March to December. They have summer vacation in December, January, and February. Many city schools have two shifts during the day. Kids go to class from eight in the morning to noon or from one o'clock to five o'clock. In country areas, you can find one- or two-room schoolhouses with just one or two teachers for all the grades.

▲ *Schoolkids in their white smocks pal around before class begins in Córdoba, a city in the center of Argentina.*

What We Do for Fun

For birthday parties and for holidays, families get together for a parrilla barbecue. Chess is a favorite board game for many kids. Sports are big, too. Soccer is tops for playing and watching. Argentina's pro teams are world famous. Rugby, basketball, tennis, and field hockey are played by lots of kids as well as by pro teams. Argentina won the field hockey Women's World Cup in 2002. **Pato**, another popular sport, is like polo and basketball combined. Players on horseback try to get a six-handled ball into a high basket. Argentina's cities, especially Buenos Aires, where there are museums, movies, malls, parks, and theaters, offer plenty of other things to do.

◀ *The tango is the national dance of Argentina.*

Garsh, I keep stepping on my tails when I dance!

Imagine the sound the water makes as it roars over the falls! ▲

Holidays and Celebrations

Christmas and New Year's are favorite warm-weather holidays. In Buenos Aires, fireworks and a parade welcome the New Year. Carnaval is held in the spring, with costume parades and dance parties. Water-balloon fights are part of the fun. It's hard to stay dry on the street during Carnaval! When girls turn fifteen they get a special party to celebrate growing up. Some families even host a fancy dress-up dance party. Boys have to wait until they are eighteen to celebrate being grown up. Their parties are much simpler—a barbecue or just going out with friends. Argentines also enjoy some regional festivals. On the coast, there is a yearly Fish Harvest celebration. People dressed as sea creatures parade. Buenos Aires hosts a livestock show and fiesta in July. In June, there is a gaucho parade with folk artists in Salta, in the northwest cattle country.

▼ *Gauchos on horseback dress in their traditional capes and hats for a festival.*

Over-the-Top Falls

The Iguaçú Falls lie on the border between Argentina and Brazil. The falls form a huge, two-and-a-half-mile horseshoe shape at the top of a cliff. Water from the Iguaçú River tumbles over the cliff in a series of 275 separate falls. Some of the falls hit ledges as they go and send up sprays of mist. Still others head straight down about 270 feet. That's the height of a twenty-four-story high-rise building! The sound of the water roars like thunder that won't stop. When the water hits bottom it sends up enormous mists. The mists are like a constant tropical rain, helping the rain forest grow along the edges of the falls and the river. The rain forest is home to yellow-beaked toucans, macaws, and other tropical birds, all sorts of snakes, tree frogs, and orchids, and the coati, a relative of the raccoon (but with a longer tail and a pointed snout). For many years the rain forest in the region of the falls was being cut down to make way for farms and ranches, but now the forest is protected as a national park.

153

Ola!

Brazil

FAST FACTS

Population:	184,101,109
Area:	3,286,487 sq. miles
Capital:	Brasilia
Languages:	Portuguese

Our nation's motto is
Order and Progress.

Practice makes
perfect! Now Pluto
can balance four balls!

Who Are We?

Brazilians come from many cultures. About half trace their heritage to Europe, while more than a third are a mix of European and African. About six in one hundred are African. Some Brazilians come from a combination of cultures and backgrounds. They may be a mixture of European, African, Native American, Middle Eastern, and Asian. (Brazil has the world's second-largest Japanese population outside Japan.) People from Portugal settled in Brazil beginning in the 1500s. Most everyone speaks Portuguese, with Native American and African words sprinkled in. Most people are Catholic, but many other faiths are practiced. One-twentieth of all Brazilians are Protestant, Jewish, Muslim, Hindu, Buddhist, or Mormon.

Brazilian kids come from a mixture of backgrounds. ▶

▲ These children hang out in a sleeping hammock, a comfy—and cool—way to sleep in the hot, muggy air along the Amazon River.

Our Communities

More people live in Brazil than in the rest of South America! Over three quarters of them crowd into Brazil's cities, which are mostly along the coast. (Much of the country's inland is farmland or rain forest.) São Paulo, in the south, is the second-largest city in the world. It has seventeen million people in its city and suburbs!

Factories produce airplanes, space satellites, cars, clothing, and computers—almost anything you can imagine. Outside the city are huge farms where oranges, coffee, and sugar are grown. Rio de Janeiro is another large city north of São Paulo. It is known for industries that make clothing, medicines, and food products. People in cities live in all kinds of housing—everything from glamorous apartments to small houses without running water. Large farms spread throughout the northeast, south, and southeast of the country. Some are ranches. Others grow sugar cane, cocoa, and coffee. Settlers in the rain forest and other interior areas grow basic crops or raise cattle on smaller pieces of cleared land. Most Native Americans live in the Amazon's rain forests. Some Amazonians live in floating houses along the river.

Our Country

No two ways about it, Brazil is huge. It's about the size of the United States, and it covers half of South America. The Andes are on the west and the Atlantic Ocean is on the east. The equator crosses Brazil in the north. Brazil borders all of the continent's countries, except for Chile and Ecuador. Brazil has a 4,600-mile-long coastline, lined with white beaches and bustling port cities like Rio de Janeiro. The Amazon River runs from west to east across the north of Brazil. It runs through the Amazon rain forest, which spreads across the northern part of the country. Below this region is an open landscape of flat rock and grassy hills, leading to low mountains in the south. In the west are swampy wetlands. Most of Brazil has a hot, tropical climate. The southern area is milder. Sometimes winter there includes frost and even snow.

▼ Rio de Janeiro sits on a beautiful bay lined with beaches.

155

What We Eat

Brazilians chow down on a diverse diet. Beans, manioc flour (farina), white rice, coconuts, palm oil, dried cod, and shrimp are common ingredients. Feijoada completa, usually made with black beans, pork, and manioc, is considered the national dish. However, each region has its own specialties. Duck in breadfruit sauce is an Amazon favorite. In Salvador, Moqueca, a seafood stew with coconut milk and palm oil, is a popular dish. The food of Rio de Janeiro and São Paulo and many other Brazilian cities is very international. Restaurants serve foods of many cultures.

Street food is enjoyed everywhere. Hungry snackers can pick up salgadinhos (spicy, filled pastries), fried bean-meal balls, or savory cakes with barbecued tidbits. Looking for a sweet? Try a Romeo and Juliet. That's a cheese and guava fruit-paste goody.

◄ *This street-food cook puts together a combo of rice, beans, and veggies.*

◄ *Some schoolkids go on field trips. This boy is visiting the Latin American Memorial, an art museum in São Paulo.*

What We Study

Many city schools have three four-hour shifts—morning, afternoon, and evening. In some very small towns, schools don't have teachers who can handle all subjects. So, some kids take classes offered on the radio. The teachers of these classes can instruct from a broadcast studio in a city. Some places have "schools on wheels" that bring teachers, books, and supplies to the kids who need them.

▼ *Time for exercise! Schoolkids wait their turn on the football field.*

What We Do for Fun

It should be easy to have fun in Brazil—the country has so much to offer! It's easy to find a beach along the coast, where many people enjoy the sun or take part in water sports. Sports of all sorts are prime. Football is a national passion. The country

▲ *Watch the moves! These boys are practicing capoeira.*

is crazy about the World Cup. Brazil has won a number of times. Street football and skateboarding are favorites. **Capoeira** is a one-of-a-kind Brazilian kick-fighting sport that started four hundred years ago. It uses dance moves as well as kicks and sweeps of the feet. Two players "fight" to music in the center of a ring. Brazil also has museums, theaters, movies, parks, and lots of places to eat. Dancing and music are part of life everywhere. Brazilian music blends Spanish, African, and Caribbean sounds.

Holidays and Celebrations

Brazil's biggest celebration, **Carnaval**, lasts three to four days just before Lent begins in early spring. (Lent is a period of six quiet weeks when Christians are supposed to prepare for Easter.) **Carnaval** is Brazil's last big party before settling down to Lent. People prepare all year. Neighborhoods put together their own bands, floats, and dance groups for the celebration. Wild costumes, decked-out floats, dancing, and parades are all part of the street carnival. **Carnaval** in Rio de Janeiro is so famous that people come from all over the world to see it. The rest of the year is filled with smaller celebrations. Almost every town has its own saint's day celebration. This often includes a small parade to carry a statue or picture of the saint through the streets. The festival of Our Lady of the Winds and Storms takes place in the seaside city of Salvador. It includes washing the statue and the steps of its church. At high tide, flowers and perfume are brought to honor the saint.

Tee-hee, I have the best hat for Carnaval!

Some Carnaval costumes take a year to make. ▶

Living Large on the Amazon

Travelers on the Amazon River turn up some of the biggest and most unusual members of the animal world. One animal you don't want to trip over on the river's edge is the anaconda python, which can be thirty feet long, weigh up to 550 pounds, and be a foot thick! This reptile is not poisonous, but instead kills its prey by grabbing hold with its teeth and dragging it into the water where the anaconda lives. The snake wraps itself tightly around its prey and squeezes until it dies.

Anacondas have a healthy appetite. They have been known to eat capybaras, deer, and jaguars— whole! The snake manages this feat because it has a jaw that can be unhinged to allow its mouth to fit easily around the prey's head.

Then the snake's powerful muscles help swallow the prey, which can take many hours. The snake also takes a long time to digest its food. After a big meal, the snake may not eat again for many days.

It's not so hard to see this anaconda on a dry gravel background. Picking it out in the waters of the Amazon or along plant-covered shores is another thing! Its yellow or green skin and brown-black patterns usually help it blend into its rain forest home.▼

Pura Vida!

Hi!

Costa Rica

FAST FACTS

Population: 3,956,507
Area: 19,730 sq. miles
Capital: San José
Language: Spanish

Our country's national anthem is "National Hymn of Costa Rica."

Hey, Donald! Everyone is ready to march!

Who Are We?

Most Costa Ricans have European ancestors, with the majority of them being from Spain. When Spanish settlers first came here, they found few groups of Native Americans. There is a small group of mestizos, or people of mixed Spanish and Native American heritage. The mestizos and European descendants add up to ninety-four of every hundred Costa Ricans. There is also a small black community descended from Jamaican immigrants. Spanish is the country's official language. Three quarters of the country is Catholic and another tenth is Protestant. There is also a small Jewish community in San José.

With two seacoasts, mountains, and a rain forest, kids in Costa Rica see a lot of wildlife, such as this marine turtle coming ashore to lay its eggs. ▶

Our Country

Costa Rica is home to a large variety of the earth's species of plants and animals. There are more than 3,000 kinds of butterflies, 850 kinds of birds, 209 species of mammals, and 10,000 different kinds of plants. Costa Rica is on a neck of land between Mexico and South America. The Pacific Ocean is on the west, and the Caribbean Sea is on the east. Four volcanic mountain ranges run north to south along the interior. Dense tropical rain forests grow on the Caribbean coastal lowlands. The Caribbean coast has tropical rains and warmer temperatures, while mountain areas are cooler.

◀ *Many houses in Costa Rica are built to take advantage of the warm climate. Air circulates under the house. The roof hangs over far enough to give shade and let rain pour off away from the house.*

Our Communities

Costa Ricans call themselves "Ticos." Why? Some people say it's because they are very enthusiastic, and use a lot of words like fanta*tico* and simpa*tico*. Most live in the country's central highlands, where the climate is mild. The capital, San José, is in a central valley in the highlands. A third of the population lives in city neighborhoods called **barrios**. About half the country's population lives outside the cities on farms or in towns. Some live in adobe farmhouses with tile roofs. Coffee, bananas, sugarcane, and cocoa are major crops. Raising cattle is also important. Quaker dairy farmers founded Monteverde and its preserved rain forest in the northwest. Nature-loving tourists come to visit these protected areas.

San José is a modern city, with a mix of high-rise buildings and single-family homes. ▶

159

What We Eat

Fruits and veggies take center stage in Costa Rican meals. As in other Latin American countries, rice and beans are served with many meals. Many types of squash, like zucchini and chayote, are added to beef, fish, or chicken dishes. Gallos are tortillas stuffed with mashed black beans, cheese, or meat. Gallo pinto is a breakfast mix of rice, beans, and onions. Ceviche—a dish of raw seafood marinated in lime juice—is another favorite. Corn shows up in lots of recipes. A soup called pozole and pancakes called chorreadas are made with corn.

Cities and towns in seaside areas have lots of snack bars and fast-food places serving burgers and pizza, too.

◀ Plantain—a kind of banana—is sliced and deep-fried to make patacones—a great snack or side dish.

What We Study

Half the primary schools in Costa Rica are one-room schoolhouses in country villages and towns. They serve one-tenth of Costa Rica's grade-school kids. The rest of the country's kids go to schools in cities and suburbs. These schools have a classroom and a teacher for each grade. Kids wear uniforms. Grade school lasts for six years. Then kids go to a three-year middle school. After that they may choose another two years of school to prepare for college or a technical job. Many businesses based in the United States are opening offices and factories in Costa Rica. The government has decided that all schools should teach English and computer skills to prepare students for work.

▼ School's out! These boys carry their homework in backpacks.

▲ Kids enjoy San Jose's Children's Museum—the fact that the building used to be a prison doesn't stop anyone from having fun!

What We Do For Fun

Costa Ricans have a lot of fun in the sun. There are two seacoasts with beautiful beaches. No one in Costa Rica is more than one hundred miles or so from a beach! Costa Rica also has some lovely inland lakes. It's no wonder that surfing, sailing, fishing, and windsurfing are very popular. Other popular sports and events include horseback riding, bicycling, bowling, rodeos, and bullfights. Soccer, of course, is at the top of the sports list.

Cities, especially San José, offer lots of fun. There are department stores, malls, and lively markets for shopping. Museums show off Costa Rica's art. Kids can see lots of movies, mostly foreign films from Mexico, Europe, and the United States. Popular Costa Rican folk music is played on the **marimba**, a kind of xylophone. Radio stations play music from around the world. Rock, rap, calypso, salsa—you name it, they play it!

Holidays and Celebrations

It seems Costa Ricans have a festival for everything! There's a corn festival, when people dress in costumes made of husks, grains, and corn silk. There's a coffee festival that includes a coffee-picking tournament. With one-fifth of the people working in farming, it's no wonder there's a Farmer's Day. There's even an Oxcart Drivers' Day with a parade of colorful carts.

December is a monthlong celebration in Costa Rica, leading up to the big night, Christmas Eve. In late-December San Jose celebrates with the **Tope**, a parade of horsemen and horsewomen from all over the country. The

▲ *These beautifully painted oxcarts were once used to haul crops from the fields. Today they are mostly used for special events.*

I'm on my way to the festival of the day— I just hope I can stop when I get there!

parade also features dancers, bands, and Costa Rica's famous oxcarts. For nine days leading up to Christmas, many families celebrate the **Posadas**. Each night they gather at a different house to sing carols, eat, and look forward to Christmas. Kids sometimes dress up as shepherds and go house to house, singing. They represent the shepherds who visited the stable in Bethlehem at the first Christmas.

Look Out Below!

What's the best way to get a look at some of the monkeys, hummingbirds, tree frogs, and snakes that live in the Costa Rican rain forest? Many of the most unusual animals spend their entire lives at the top, or canopy, of the jungle. The only way to get a close-up look is to walk along the treetops! Visitors to the forest can walk on suspended walkways strung for miles at the top of the forest, or hang on for dear life to zip lines that swing them through the canopy!

▲ *These visitors to the rain forest get a treetop view on a canopy walkway.*

Some tree frogs spend most of their lives in the canopies and never visit the ground. ▶

Hi!

Hola!

FAST FACTS

Population:	104,959,594
Area:	761,602 sq. miles
Capital:	Mexico City
Language:	Spanish

162

Who Are We?

More people live in Mexico than in any other Latin American country except Brazil. Almost a third of Mexico's population is Native American. Native Americans in Mexico can trace their roots back to powerful cultures such as the Toltecs, Aztecs, or Mayans. Mestizos (a mix of Native Americans and Spanish) make up two-thirds of the population. European descendants make up most of the rest of the population. Spanish is the official language of Mexico. Most Mexicans are Roman Catholic. Some Native Americans combine Catholicism with traditional Native American beliefs. Smaller numbers of people are Protestant or Jewish.

This boy from Chihuahua, in Mexico's cowboy country, gets ready to board a train that can take him all the way to the Pacific Coast. Along the way it goes through desert, mountains, and across amazing, deep canyons. ▶

▲ *San Miguel de Allende is a city that has preserved buildings from its Spanish colonial days.*

Our Country

Mexico is in the northern part of Latin America. The United States is its neighbor to the north. Guatemala and Belize lie to the south. Mexico has rain forests, beautiful beaches, and desert. The heart of the country is a high plateau, where some of Mexico's major cities are located. Two large mountain chains range along each side of the plateau. South of this are the Central Highlands. Mexico City, the country's capital, is in a large valley located in these highlands. In the north, and in the mountains and highlands, the climate is temperate and mostly dry. In the south and along the coast the weather is often hot and wet.

Our Communities

Three out of four Mexicans live in cities. People living in the cities work in industries that produce cars, metal products, clothing, chemicals, and food products. Many Mexicans work in service jobs in hotels, restaurants, stores, schools, hospitals, and offices. Mexico City is the oldest city in North America. More than sixteen million people live in and around this extremely modern city, which has huge skyscrapers, graceful old Spanish buildings, and ruins of Aztec temples, all in the same neighborhoods. Mexico City also has many residential areas on its outskirts made up of thousands of very simple brick houses. About one fifth of all Mexicans work in farming and ranching. Many live on small farms called ejidos.

▼ *In Mexico City, there is one stadium for bullfights and one for soccer.*

What We Eat

Native Americans made corn the star ingredient of Mexican food. It is a part of almost every traditional meal. Tamales are made of cornmeal steamed in a corn husk. Tortillas are Mexico's daily bread. They are flat, thin disks made of cornmeal mixed with water and baked and can be stuffed with chicken, meat, or beans. They can be fried into tacos. When sandwiched around spicy cheese, they are called quesadillas.

The Native Americans of Mexico also gave the world chocolate, tomatoes, and vanilla. The Spaniards brought rice, meat, and spices. Today, these staples make up a large part of the Mexican diet. Meat dishes are common in the northern cities and towns. Seafood dishes are popular on the coasts. Mole, a famous sauce made from many ground spices and vegetables, comes from Oaxaca in the south.

◀ Salsas—spicy mixes of tomato, chiles, cilantro, and spice—are a popular dip for tortillas.

▲ Boy dreaming of his future in a classroom

What We Study

In many country areas, one or two teachers cover all the grades. Some of these schools have lessons beamed in on TV sets. The teacher is in a TV studio in a city, teaching kids in small schools around the country. Kids learn the same advanced science or math that the kids in large city schools are learning. Kids are required to go to school through ninth grade, although some students leave school early to help their families by earning money.

After Minnie, I love soccer best!

What We Do for Fun

In a big country like Mexico, with beaches and mountains and cities, there are many ways to have fun. Soccer is popular. So are baseball, rugby, horseback riding, and **jai alai**. Jai alai is a kind of handball played with a handwoven, curved basket, called a **cesta**, that is strapped to players' arms and used to catch and throw the ball. Bullfighting is also big, and there are more than 225 bullrings around the country.

There are many museums, parks, and colonial sites to visit. In nice weather, families often spend Sundays in Mexico's parks. Mexico makes its own movies and TV programs, and kids also watch movies and TV from the United States.

▲ Every region of Mexico has its own dance style and music. Lots of kids—boys and girls—learn the steps and the music.

▼ Cannonball! These kids play at the beach resort of Cancun.

Holidays and Celebrations

Mexico has many festivals celebrating harvests, saints' days, and patriotic occasions. Most feature street fairs with food, dancing, and mariachi bands of guitarists, trumpet players, singers, and dancers. Mexican Independence Day is September 16, but the celebrating gets started the night before. At 11 P.M., the president of Mexico stands on a balcony in the main square of Mexico City, where up to a million people have gathered. He calls out the "Cry of Dolores," words a Mexican patriot used in 1810 to rally the people to fight against Spanish rule. He ends with the words *Viva Mexico* (Long live Mexico). The crowd roars the words back and the celebration gets underway with fireworks and a full night of parties. The next day brings a huge parade, more parties, and family celebrations.

◄ *The first two days of November are Dias de los Muertos—Days of the Dead—when many Mexicans remember relatives who have died. They visit the graves, decorate them with marigolds and candles, and leave offerings of food and candy shaped like skeletons.*

The Mystery of the Pyramids

The ancient people of Mexico built a lot of pyramids. Just outside Mexico City stand the ruins of the ancient city of Teotihuacán, built around two thousand years ago. By about 300 A.D., this city was the sixth largest in the world. It had about 200,000 people living in it, and it was a center of trade, farming, religion, and government. The most famous structures in Teotihuacán are the Pyramid of the Sun and the Pyramid of the Moon. These buildings were probably used as temples or observatories. Smaller pyramids in the city were apartment-style housing for people who worked and lived there. The city thrived for almost one thousand years. Then, by 700 A.D., the people seem to have disappeared. Today's scientists have found evidence that a huge fire swept through the city and burned down all but the stone buildings. What happened? Was the fire an accident? Did invaders burn the city? Why did the people leave forever? Why didn't they return to rebuild? Who were these people in the first place? They left no writing and no history. The only clues are their mysterious pyramids.

Scientists are carefully digging into the pyramids of Teotihuacán and examining them to learn as much as they can about the people who built them. ►

Hi!

Hola!
Winchis!

Peru

FAST FACTS

Population:	27,544,305
Area:	496,223 sq. miles
Capital:	Lima
Languages:	Spanish and Quechua

Our nation's motto is Liberty and Order.

There's no freer feeling than this, eh, Goofy?

Who Are We?

Most Peruvians today are at least part Aymara or Quechua Native Americans. More than a third are mestizo (a mix of European and Native American). People whose families came from Europe make up about one-sixth of the population. (Most of those families came from Spain.) Smaller numbers of people with African, Chinese, or Japanese heritage also live in Peru. Most Peruvians are Roman Catholic. About a tenth of the people are Protestant, Jewish, or Muslim.

Peru has two official languages: Spanish and Quechua, an ancient Native American language. There are about seventy different Native American languages, each spoken by a small group.

Native American girls wear nice hats like these in the cold Andes Mountains. ▶

▲ *Much of Peru's farming takes place on its beautiful highlands.*

Our Communities

Peru's population is divided between its coastal cities, the highlands, and the Amazon basin. The coastal region is where Peru does most of its business. Manufacturing and port cities provide work for residents. Farmers grow cotton, rice, sugarcane, fruits, and vegetables in the coastal plain, and there are vineyards as well. A quarter of all Peruvians crowd into Lima, and more keep coming. Many small native groups live in the isolated Amazon rain forest and survive by hunting, fishing, and growing crops. Iquitos is Peru's largest city in the Amazon basin. The only way to get there is by plane or boat—there are no roads.

▼ *Lima is a city with many squares and parks, old Spanish-style buildings, and new high-rises.*

Our Country

Peru is situated on the western side of South America. It has many climate areas—dry coastal deserts and icy, snowcapped mountains. Lima, the capital city, sits midway down the flat, coastal plain. This narrow plain includes deserts, farmland, fishing villages, and oil fields. The central mountain area has massive peaks, plateaus, and steep canyons. Ancient Incan ruins are found here. Dense forest lies east of the Andes and slopes down to the Amazon's rain forest and plains.

What We Eat

In Peru, what goes on the table often depends on where the table is. Ceviche, raw seafood marinated in lime juice, salt, and pepper, is a seaside specialty. In the highlands, people eat mostly meat and potatoes (or rice). In the Amazon rain forest, freshwater fish and tropical fruits are typical. Rice, corn, and potatoes are basics everywhere. Chicken, pork, and lamb are the principal meats. Cuy, grilled guinea pig, is a dish you won't find in many places outside Peru. Pachamanca ("cooked underground") is a style of cooking that goes back five hundred years. Cooks wrap potatoes, meat, and vegetables in leaves and cook the food under hot rocks in a dug-out pit.

◄ Native American farmers bring their goods to sell at city markets, like this one in Pisac, near Cuzco.

What We Study

Every small village has an **escuelita**, a "little school." Volunteers from the village often build the one-room schools, which usually have one teacher to take care of all the grades. In some villages, the teacher is the most educated person in the town and is given a lot of respect. In the countryside, there aren't many high schools, so students who want to continue their education may have to travel a long distance every day.

Many city schools are very big, with many students. Kids who finish high school may take an extra year to study for a test that will get them into one of Peru's universities.

▼ School groups get to see their ancient history up close on trips to Incan ruins.

▲ Splashdown: these girls swim in an oasis lagoon set smack in the middle of Peru's driest desert area.

What We Do for Fun

Peruvian kids are nuts for soccer! They also play and watch pro volleyball and basketball teams. Along the coast, many kids enjoy water sports such as surfing, rafting, snorkeling, and sailing. Hikers and climbers head for the mountains. Many Peruvian kids enjoy board games like chess and sapo, which was probably invented by Spanish settlers. Today's game board features a brass frog with an open mouth. Players stand about fifteen to twenty-five feet from the board and toss coins at spaces on the board for points. The best possible play is to throw a coin into the frog's mouth! Peru has great museums to visit, full of Incan displays. Cities offer lots of restaurants, movie theaters, and shopping. All of Peru has great music. Musicians play everything from Andes-Mountain tunes to folk music that blends African, Native American, and Spanish sounds.

Holidays and Celebrations

There's no way anyone could take part in all of Peru's festivals: about three thousand take place every year! There are religious, patriotic, and cultural celebrations. Most are Catholic saints' day celebrations that sometimes combine Catholic and Native American traditions. The night before Cuzco's celebration of the Catholic feast of Corpus Christi, people make a point of eating twelve different dishes. On the day itself, there is a procession with statues of fifteen saints and virgins. The Native Americans of Cuzco also celebrate an ancient religious tradition called the Adoration of the Sun. There are also many Peruvian harvest celebrations. The **Yunza** festival includes a celebration around a tree covered with gifts. Couples dance around, cutting at the tree until it falls. The couple that finally makes the tree fall is in charge of organizing the next Yunza event.

People of Cuzco carry the statue of a saint in a religious procession. ▲

A Stargazing Peak

Machu Picchu is an ancient city perched high in the Andes Mountains, overlooking a deep river valley. Forest vines covered it for four hundred years, until 1911, when a scientist discovered it. Ever since, the government of Peru, scientists, and historians have worked together to investigate and protect this stone city consisting of a palace, several temples, an observatory, storehouses, an open-air auditorium, and two hundred small homes. Each building is made of stone blocks placed so neatly together that no mortar was needed to keep them in place. A system of water tanks and fountains moved water through the city and watered the fields.

Machu Picchu was very advanced for its time. The city of Machu Picchu may have been a hideaway for an Incan emperor, and it was also the site of important religious ceremonies. *Intihuatana*, which means "for tying the sun," is a column of stone rising from a giant rock. As the winter solstice approached, and the sun seemed to disappear with each day, a priest would hold a ceremony trying to keep the sun from vanishing by tying it to the rock.

▼ The mysterious city of Machu Picchu was hidden in the mountains.

Mike's Travel Journal
in Latin America

Can you find me in the photos?

Knitted stripes of the Andes! ▶

Colonia Tovar, Venezuela

Time Travel

Visiting Colonia Tovar in Venezuela is like going through a cultural time warp. This 160-year-old town tucked away high in the Andes was founded in 1845 by 400 people from the Black Forest of Germany. They built homes and businesses like the ones back home, only spoke German, ate German foods, and pretty much kept to themselves. (That was easy, because there was no road to the town for almost 100 years!) Now this place is one of Venezuela's biggest tourist attractions.

Super-sized Ice Cubes

The Perito Moreno glacier is a moving river of solid ice flowing from ice fields covering the Andes Mountains along Argentina's border with Chile. The glacier moves, bit by bit, until it reaches Lake Argentina. At that point, the glacier's front edge is a 180-foot-high curtain of blue ice a mile and a half wide! Huge chunks of the ice break off and fall into the lake with a roaring sound like thunder. (Why is the ice blue? Glacier ice has been put under pressure for thousands of years, so it is extra heavy and thick. It reflects only blue light and absorbs all other colors.)

Perito Moreno glacier, Argentina

◀ Coffee

Mystery Lines

Imagine enormous designs carved into the floor and hillsides of a Peruvian desert. There are drawings of animals, people, flowers, and objects like this one that some people call the candelabra. Others are just shapes like triangles, rectangles, and spirals. Each design is so huge that you can't see the whole thing or tell what it looks like unless you look at it from high in the air. But these carvings are almost 2,000 years old! There were no airplanes or skyscrapers then. What were these designs for? Who got to see them—and how? How on earth were they made? Some scientists think the lines were made for religious ceremonies; others think they may have something to do with astronomy. But no one really knows.

Peru

Up Close and Personal—with a Whale

San Ignacio Bay on the west coast of Mexico is a nursery for gray whales. The huge whales spend their summers along the coast of Alaska, but in winter they head to the waters off Mexico for the warmer weather. Pregnant females give birth in San Ignacio Bay, where they spend the winter rearing their babies, getting them ready for the trek north in spring. Visitors can go out in small boats to see the whales, and sometimes the whales come right up to the boats! Some of these mammals seem to be as curious about people as people are about them.

San Ignacio Bay, Mexico

Lava Land

Costa Rica is a land of 100 volcanoes. Luckily, only a few are likely to erupt or explode any time soon. Irazu, the biggest of Costa Rica's volcanoes, has two craters or bowl-shaped openings on top. One is filled with water that turns colors from the volcano's chemicals and minerals. Some days the water is red—and some days it's green! On a clear day, both the Atlantic and Pacific can be seen from Irazu's top. When Irazu erupted in 1963, it continued to throw up gas and ash for two years! People miles away, in San José, had to carry umbrellas and wear masks to avoid the bits of ash that rained down.

Look at these coins! There are pre-Columbian patterns on them. ▶

Costa Rica

If You Lived Here

Home, community, food, school, fun, celebrations, places to visit, and more! Kids all around the world have so many common experiences. Here's how kids in Latin America might enjoy a few more things familiar to many kids around the globe—as well as a peek at some unique events!

Happy Birthday!

In Argentina, friends give your earlobe a tug for every year—and one to grow on!

A Latin American girl's fifteenth birthday is an extra special big dance party with friends and relatives. This is when she's considered a grown-up.

At birthday parties in **Mexico** and other Latin American countries, a fancy papier mâché container (usually in the shape of an animal), called a piñata, is filled with candies and small treats, and hoisted high in the air on a rope. Partygoers are blindfolded, given a stick, and aim at the piñata, taking turns to break it open and release the treats inside.

> Going to get candy from piñata NOW!

What an Event!

> I bet I could surfboard all the way through the Panama Canal!

How do you paddle a canoe from the Atlantic Ocean to the Pacific Ocean in less than two days? When you race through the Panama Canal! There's a race especially for teenagers, where they paddle along in thirty-foot-long dugout canoes.

Carnival in **Venezuela** is a winter festival filled with parties, music, and water balloons!

Friends try to drench each other, all in the spirit of fun.

On December 23rd, the city of Oaxaca, **Mexico,** celebrates the Night of the Radish. The central square is decorated with figures carved from giant radishes. The tradition began 100 years ago, when farmers carved the veggies to attract people to a Christmas market.

The Family Pet

Birds are the most popular pets in **Argentina**.

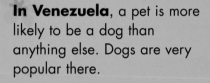

> Stitch, you're better than any dog!

In Venezuela, a pet is more likely to be a dog than anything else. Dogs are very popular there.

North America

Howdy!
Let's giddy-up and
see the sights!

GREENLAND

ALASKA
UNITED STATES OF AMERICA

CANADA

UNITED STATES
OF AMERICA

FAST FACTS

Population: 325,535,445
Area: 7,048,458 sq. miles
Countries: 2

Come along and visit
North America!

These neighboring countries have diverse lands, wildlife, and people.

What kind of kids can you meet? In the far north above the Arctic Circle, a Native American Inuit girl might show you how to drive a dogsled. In the subways of Montreal, Canada, you could sit next to kids talking in French about ice hockey. You could exchange a wave with an African American teen on his way to band practice in Seattle, Washington, in the United States, or go horseback riding at a Manitoba, Canada, ranch with an eleven-year-old boy after he finishes Hebrew school. Maybe you'll meet a girl who moved to Massachusetts from Brazil so her father could join her uncle's fishing business. You could have dinner in Houston, Texas, in the high-rise apartment of a Vietnamese-American family.

The People

The people of Canada and the United States come from all over the world and make up five percent of the world's population. The first to settle these lands were ancestors of today's Native Americans. Then, over 500 years ago, first explorers, and then waves of settlers from Europe, began coming. Over time, Africans, Asians, and Latin Americans also came to these countries.

These North Americans do all kinds of work and make all kinds of products—everything from cars and airplanes to computer games and lifesaving medicines. They make movies and print magazines and write hip-hop music. Farms and ranches here are important sources of food for many parts of the world.

▼ Ridgeway, Colorado, U.S.A., Last Dollar Ranch

The Land

▲ *Lac O'Hara, Canada*

Canada and the United States take up the northern two thirds of North America. Between them, they have almost every type of land you can imagine: glacier-covered mountains, swamps and marshlands, river deltas, deserts, rolling plains, immense forests, and rain forests. Canada and Alaska (a state in the United States), reach far up into the icy Arctic Ocean. The middle of both countries is made up of long, rolling plains—good for growing grains and raising cattle. Here there are cold winters and short, hot, dry summers. The coasts of both countries have warmer, wetter weather than their interiors. Canada alone has more than 2,000,000 lakes! It shares four of the five Great Lakes with the United States. The St. Lawrence River Seaway connects the lakes to the Atlantic Ocean. Most of Canada's largest cities are strung along its southern border with the United States. The United States is sandwiched between Canada in the north and Mexico, the Caribbean, and the Gulf of Mexico in the south.

> See Buzz, this land sure beats anything in outer space!

The Animals

Polar bears roam the icy Arctic Circle. Alaska and Canada's northern shores are also icy playgrounds for puffin birds and seals. Caribou, a type of reindeer, also thrive in the Arctic. Wolves, foxes, and bobcats hunt their dinner on prairies and plains of both countries. Blue heron and Canadian geese are some of Canada's 500 types of birds. The bald eagle (the national symbol of the United States) lives only in North America. The gray coyote, once endangered, has rebounded in many parts of the United States and Canada. Rattlesnakes live in the hot, dry Southwest desert. Pink flamingos wade Florida's everglade waters. Whales surface in the waters along both coasts.

ATTENTION!

▲ *Moose crossing road sign*

The Environment

Acid rain is a problem that Canada and the United States share. It is caused when coal, gasoline, or oil is burned, sending sulfur dioxide or nitrogen oxide into the air, where they mix with moisture. The rain or snow made from this combination can eat away at solid rock! (Acid rain falling in cities can wear away the features of statues and the bricks of buildings.) When it gets into lakes and rivers, acid rain can poison fish and plants. When it is absorbed into the earth, it can hurt the soil's ability to grow plants.

Canada has been taking steps to control the amount of gases companies send into the air. The United States has made cutbacks too, but with many industries and power plants near the Canadian border, the winds blow acid rain into Canada! The two governments are looking for a solution.

175

Hi!

Hi!

Bonjour !

Canada

Canada is this big!

FAST FACTS

Population: 32,507,874
Area: 3,855,081 sq. miles
Capital: Ottawa
Languages: English and French

Our nation's motto is
From Sea to Sea.

Who Are We?

Canadians come from all over the world. About one-quarter have roots in the United Kingdom. Another quarter is of French heritage. About one in fifty Canadians is Native American or Inuit (people who live in the far north, near or above the Arctic Circle). The French were the first Europeans to settle in Canada, putting down roots in the eastern part of the country, where most French-Canadians still live today. People from Great Britain settled in the rest of the country. About eighty-five out of every hundred Canadians are Christian. Most other Canadians are Jewish, Hindu, or Muslim.

Fisherwoman with a northen pike, caught while ice fishing in northern Alberta ▶

Our Country

▲ *Niagara Falls, Canadian side*

Canada is derived from a Native American word that means "village." It's the second largest country on the planet, and is divided into ten provinces and three territories. Canada has only one neighbor, the United States, and it stretches across six time zones east to west, from the Atlantic to the Pacific, reaching far north into the frozen Arctic Ocean. Its landscape is a mix of prairie grasslands, wetlands, frozen earth in the Arctic, and high, rugged mountain ranges. Forest covers much of the country. The Cordillera Mountain range runs along the western edge. The Rocky Mountains begin here before they run south into the United States. East of the Rockies are lowlands and plains. The Great Lakes, Niagara Falls, and the St. Lawrence Seaway are in the central south, which is an area of farmland and industrial centers. There are year-round snow and ice fields in the far north.

Our Communities

Eighty percent of Canada's 32 million people live in cities that are strung like beads on a necklace within 130 miles of Canada's border with the United States. Most Canadians live in cities, in houses or apartments. Vancouver, a thriving city on the west coast, is one of North America's largest ports and home to many movie and television production companies. Ottawa is the country's capital and home to many government

workers. Montreal is the largest French-speaking city in the world after Paris. Many people living outside cities, especially in the west and the far north, work in the oil industry, and in forestry, farming, ranching, fishing, hunting, or mining.

The city of Vancouver ▼

What We Eat

How about some flapper pie? That's what western Canadians call banana or coconut cream pie. Maybe you'd like a taste of Jigg's Dinner, what people in Newfoundland call a boiled dinner of salted meat, cabbage, and other veggies. For a really messy snack, try poutine—a French word meaning "mushy mess." And that's what this dish of fries covered in melted cheese and spicy gravy looks like!

Canada's cooks make the most of their local foods. In Newfoundland you can eat grilled Arctic char, a local fish; while out west, British Columbians enjoy lots of salmon. People in Alberta sometimes dine on venison (deer or elk meat). Maple syrup is a Quebec specialty. In spring, Montrealers pour hot syrup all over ice, roll it all up with sticks, and make maple lollipops! Immigrants to Canada bring their own favorite foods with them, so you can get everything from Greek pastries to Chinese-style roast duck.

▲ This girl snacks on a popular Canadian pastry, called beaver tail.

What We Study

Each province or territory has its own school system. All kids have to go to school until their late teens. (About three quarters graduate.) Depending on which province they live in, kids start school at age five, six, or seven. There are all sorts of schools in Canada, from one-room schoolhouses in tiny northern settlements to enormous city schools and sprawling suburban schools with grassy lawns. Schools generally teach French-speaking kids in French and English-speaking kids in English. Inuit and Native American kids sometimes go to schools that teach in their home languages. New immigrants can take classes in their original languages until they are ready to move into French- or English-speaking classrooms.

Inuit girls in a seventh-grade computer class at the Ataguttaaluk school in Igloolik, Nunavut. ▶

What We Do for Fun

Ice hockey is a national craze. Kids learn at a young age, grown-ups have amateur leagues, and everyone follows the professional teams! Kids also play team sports like basketball, volleyball, Canadian football, soccer, and baseball. Canadians make the most of their northern climate, as well as their lakes, mountains, rivers, forests, and seacoasts. Popular water sports include canoeing, kayaking, rafting, fishing, swimming, and windsurfing. The mountains and forests attract hikers, campers, mountain climbers, and skiers. Sledders, tobogganers, and skaters are everywhere. In warmer seasons, in-line skaters and skateboarders cruise around. Cities and towns, with restaurants, museums, movies, and parks, offer lots to do. And for couch potatoes, there is, of course, TV and the computer.

◀ Farm children playing ice hockey on a sunny winter day in front of a red barn, Manitoba.

Holidays and Celebrations

A canoe race on ice? Snow bathing? It must be Winter Carnival in Quebec City! For two weeks each winter, everybody celebrates with parades, dogsled rides, contests, and even costume balls. Many cities in Canada have similar winter breaks. Ottawa has its Winterlude. British Columbia offers Winterstart.

Many provinces in Canada have celebrations that reflect the culture of the region. The Calgary Stampede takes place in Alberta, Canada's cow country. It's a ten-day series of rodeos, races, cattle sales, and parties. In Toronto, Ontario's many immigrants from the Caribbean islands have created Caribana, a street carnival with food, music, and West Indian dancing.

Ice sculpture, Quebec City, Canada ▶

▲ *Salmon fishing boat, Johnstone Straight, BC, Canada*

Fish Tale

When European explorer John Cabot landed in Newfoundland around 1500, the waters were crowded with cod. According to one story, Cabot claimed they blocked his ship! True or not, the fact is that for hundreds of years, cod ruled. Fishermen came from around the world to fish off Newfoundland's shores, and a successful fishery developed there as well. Then in the 1950s, bigger boats or "factory ships" from Europe, Russia, and Cuba replaced the smaller ones. These enormous ships had huge nets that swept the ocean all the way to the bottom, dragging up whole schools of fish. They damaged much of the habitat for bottom-dwelling sea creatures, and caught so much cod that the numbers declined drastically. In 1976, the Canadian government banned foreign ships from fishing off Newfoundland's shores. Unfortunately, it didn't set limits on how many fish Canadians could take, so they built their own huge "draggers." Finally, the government had to ban all fishing off Newfoundland's shores in order to give the fish a chance to rebound.

There's nothing fishy going on here!

179

Hi!

Hi!

United States

FAST FACTS

Population:	293,027,571
Area:	3,718,780 sq. miles
Capital:	Washington, D.C.
Languages:	English

Our nation's motto is
In God We Trust.

To Infinity and Beyond!

Who Are We?

The First People

Around 20,000 years ago, ancestors of today's Native Americans crossed the land and ice that once connected Asia to what is now Alaska. Over the centuries, these first Americans developed many cultures, groups, and nations, including the Navajo, Hopi, Utes, Iroquois, and Mohawks.

Petroglyphs decorate rocks around a spring in Utah. ▶

A Big Change

In the 1500s an enormous change occurred. Europeans began to explore and settle in regions where these Native American groups were already living.

The Spanish founded the first European city in North America—St. Augustine, Florida. The British and Dutch set up colonial cities such as New York, Philadelphia, Williamsburg, and Boston. The French founded New Orleans.

The British colonies won independence from England in 1783, and gradually the new country expanded west, adding land by purchases or through war. The United States grew until it spanned from the Atlantic to the Pacific.

And They Kept Coming!

Many people came here for a new life with new opportunities. However, the first people from Africa did not come of their own free will, but were enslaved and brought here to work by Europeans. Finally, in 1865 slavery was abolished, and over time, African Americans began to gain the same opportunities as others. Today, many people from African countries come to the United States, all by choice.

Commuters riding subway car—Brooklyn, New York ▶

People Today

Three quarters of all people here have roots in Europe. Latin Americans and African Americans each make up about a tenth of the population. About one in twenty-five Americans has roots in Asia, and one in every one hundred people is Native American. Over half of all Americans are Protestant, followed by Roman Catholics, Jews, Hindus, Muslims, Buddhists, and people of other faiths. English is the official language, but a large minority speak Spanish. A number of Native American languages are also spoken. And recent newcomers still speak hundreds of different languages.

181

Our Country

From Sea to Shining Sea

Forty-eight states and the capital district, Washington, D.C., span from the Atlantic to the Pacific and make up what is called the continental United States. Continental states are often described as being part of regions, like the Northeast, Midwest, and Pacific Northwest. Alaska and Hawaii are the only states not attached to the rest. Hawaii, far out in the Pacific, is the world's longest chain of islands. Alaska, the northernmost and largest state in the United States, is separated from the "lower 48" by Canada.

◀ *The beautiful shoreline of Kauai island, Hawaii*

What the Land Looks Like

There are three main mountain ranges in the United States. The Appalachians swing up along the East Coast, from Alabama in the south all the way into Canada. The Sierra Nevada lines the West Coast. The towering Rocky Mountains stretch north into Canada and Alaska, and south almost into Mexico. Between the Appalachians and the Rockies most of the land is plains or low, rolling hills. Much of the Southwest is desert. The country is also blessed with many lakes and rivers. More than 800 rivers flow through it, including the Mississippi, one of the world's longest. Much of the land is good for farming.

Farmer standing in a wheat field during harvest time ▶

All Over the (Weather) Map

The United States has many different climate and weather zones, but most of it is temperate, with four distinct seasons. Along the Canadian border the winters are long and cold. In the South, winters are short and usually mild. In Florida the climate is almost tropical. The main mountain ranges get lots of snow in winter, and so do the plains. The rest of the year, the plains are fairly dry. Summers in the South and in the mid-Atlantic are hot and humid. The Southwest is hot and dry. The Pacific Northwest and New England summers are pretty warm. Hawaii has a tropical climate, and most of Alaska has a fairly harsh, cold climate.

◀ *Spring snow—Crater Lake National Park, Oregon*

Our Communities

All Across the Country

Many people live in cities and their surrounding suburbs along the Atlantic, Pacific, and Gulf coasts. New York City has the most people, with eight million, followed by Los Angeles, Chicago, and Houston. The Great Plains (which extend west from the Mississippi River), most western mountain states, and many parts of the Southwest are much less densely settled.

In Hawaii and Alaska, most people live along the coast in cities and towns. Some Hawaiians live in fishing villages and on farms or ranches. In Alaska, some small fishing and hunting villages scattered in the Arctic North have no roads and can be reached only by plane or boat.

Only one out of fifty Americans works in farming, ranching, or fishing. About a fifth work in industry. The rest are in service jobs of all sorts, in government, for businesses, or at hospitals, schools, stores, or restaurants.

Lifestyle

Living in and owning a house in the suburbs is very common. In cities, many people live in and often own their apartments or attached houses. Styles of housing vary greatly within a single place and across the country. Many kids in Philadelphia live in side-by-side row houses. In Seattle, some even live on houseboats! Some people prefer small-town life. Many farming and ranching communities have very small towns, with a school, a post office, and a few stores.

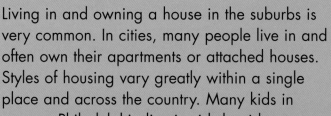

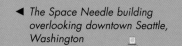

◀ The Space Needle building overlooking downtown Seattle, Washington

▲ A traditional main street of a small town

The Old Neighborhood

New immigrants to the United States who share the same language, culture, and experiences have traditionally settled in the same neighborhood. It makes the transition to a new place more comfortable. In the 1800s, many cities had neighborhoods made up of predominantly one ethnic group or another.

For instance, there were Italian, Polish, German, Irish, and Chinese neighborhoods. There are still several famous Chinatowns across the United States, including one in New York City and one in San Francisco. Many other ethnic neighborhoods still exist today, but people are mixing together more and more into the large melting pot that is the United States. In some big cities, people from more than fifty countries may be living on the same block!

What We Eat

Try It, You'll Like It!

Pizza, hamburgers, hot dogs, tacos, spaghetti, dim sum, sushi, bagels, quiche, fried squid, and pappadums. Those are just some of the favorite foods of people in the United States. The foods all come from other countries. Why not? Americans come from every place on the planet, too.

Down-Home Cooking

Americans seem to like to chow down on traditional favorites, too. New England baked beans with molasses, chicken-fried steak, cranberry sauce, Indian pudding, apple pie, succotash (lima beans and corn), popcorn, fried chicken, corn on the cob, shrimp gumbo, fudge,

▲ *A cheeseburger with "all the fixings"*

salt water taffy, tuna fish salad, and peanut butter and jelly sandwiches are all traditional foods.

Hometown Favorites

Many regions and cities of the United States have their own typical foods. In New Orleans it could be a ham, cheese, and olive sandwich on a Muffaleta roll. At baseball games in Baltimore, Maryland, you can get crab cakes instead of a hot dog. In New England, steamed lobster served with melted butter and lemon is a classic. Check out the slow-cooked barbecue beef in Texas, and the hot chilies that flavor just about everything in New Mexico. The United States was the first home of the fast-food hamburger place. Now fast-food places serving quick meals of many types are on almost every highway and in almost every town and mall.

Don't we make any burger look better?!

What We Study

School time

Most kids start kindergarten at five, and go to school until they graduate high school at eighteen. High school graduates can apply to a university or other advanced school. Through the high school years, kids can attend public schools, which are free and open to everybody. Some kids also go to religious schools or private schools. A growing number of kids study at home with their parents. This is called homeschooling.

Most grade school kids go to schools in their neighborhoods. Kids who have to travel more than a mile usually get a ride to and from school in bright yellow school buses and vans. Suburban and small-town grade schools are often one- or two-story buildings with a big playground and

sports fields. In cities, schools are often tucked in between other buildings. Instead of being low and wide, they have three to four stories. Many do not have a playground. Sometimes the police block off the street in front of city schools for play periods.

The 3 R's—and More

Kids in grade schools learn math, reading, spelling, geography, social studies, and science. Many schools also offer art, music, and physical education. Few kids in public school in the United States study a foreign language before they are twelve.

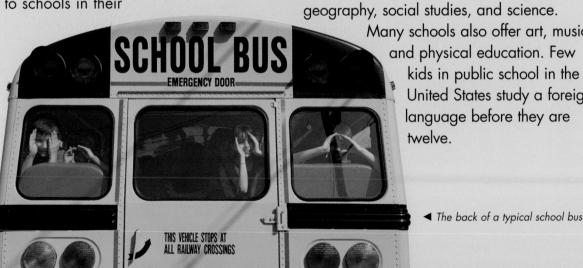

◀ *The back of a typical school bus*

What We Do for Fun

Kids Play Hard

A lot of kids play organized sports like soccer, Little League baseball, football, or basketball. They join after-school programs like scouts, take dance and music lessons, or bike or skate. Many kids are "wired"—they have home computers, telephones, and even TVs in their rooms. They spend time calling and e-mailing their friends. Computer and video games are huge! What about low-tech fun? Kids read, listen to music, play board games, and take up hobbies like collecting baseball cards or making beaded jewelry. Sleepovers are a big deal on weekends. Older kids hang out at the mall with friends.

Boy playing T-ball ▶

Sports Galore

Adults and kids alike follow many pro and university sports, especially basketball, football, and baseball. Triathlons, surf-kiting, and extreme skiing and snowboarding are becoming popular. Unlike the rest of the world, most Americans don't follow pro soccer in a big way. Americans do watch the World Cup if a United States team is in the running, and, indeed, the women's team has won several times.

◀ *Professional basketball players*

Family Fun

For vacations, which are often a week or less, families go to the beach, hike in the country, visit a big amusement park, or tour a city. During the year, they go to movies and restaurants and take day trips. Some families spend time at shopping malls on weekends. Some malls are so big they have movie theaters and amusement parks inside them!

Waterslide Park and Pool, New Jersey ▶

185

Holidays and Celebrations

Something for Everyone

Depending on their religion, Americans celebrate many holidays observed by people around the world, including Christmas, Passover, Ramadan, Diwali, and the birthday of the Buddha. There are Native American harvest and planting festivals, an African American winter holiday called Kwanzaa, and federal holidays such as Martin Luther King Day and Veterans Day.

President Bush honors Dr. Martin Luther King, Jr. ▶

Children celebrating Fourth of July ▲

Fourth of July

Americans celebrate Independence Day in honor of when American revolutionaries declared independence from England in 1776. Parades, picnics, family reunions, fireworks, and food are all part of the festivities. Hot dogs, hamburgers, corn on the cob, potato salad, and watermelon are just a few Independence Day treats.

Halloween

Irish immigrants brought along Halloween or All Hallows Eve. On October 31, the night before the Christian All Saints' Day, kids dress up like pirates, princesses, monsters, and more, and go trick-or-treating, visiting friends and neighbors to collect candy and other small treats. Even adults get in the "spirit" of things, wearing their own costumes, having parties, and decorating houses with jack-o'-lanterns (pumpkins with carved faces), skeletons, black cats, and other spooky decorations.

Thanksgiving

Now the biggest travel day of the year in the United States, this November holiday began in celebration of the settlers' first harvest in the 1600s. The biggest day for family get-togethers, many people give thanks for the good things that have happened during the year. A football game on TV and a big feast are the centerpieces of the day. In many homes, there's a big turkey dinner with stuffing, cranberry sauce, veggies, and pumpkin pie.

◀ *Family enjoying Thanksgiving dinner*

A Grand Balancing Act

A Truly Grand Canyon

Be sure to check out Echo Cliffs, Excalibur Tower, and Vulcan's Throne. Hints for a computer game? No. These are special places in the Grand Canyon, a national park that takes up more than a million acres of northwest Arizona. The Colorado River runs through the canyon, which at its deepest extends 6,000 feet down from the top. Over five million years ago, the river also ran along the top, but it slowly wore the earth away, year by year, inch by inch. At the same time, volcanoes and movements of the Earth's crust pushed some of the land upward to help create the amazing rock formations above and inside the canyon.

Colorado River, Grand Canyon National Park ▶

Sights

On a clear day you can track the winding slash of the canyon for miles. The top of the plateau has rolling, twisted forms of rock. The canyon walls have horizontal stripes of different colors. Over millions of years, layers of different rocks and minerals built up. Each layer has its own color.

Visitors

There are many ways to see the park. You can stop at lookouts along the canyon's edge, hike trails from the top to the bottom, or travel on horseback into the wilder areas. Campsites are dotted throughout the canyon. For a wild ride you could join a Colorado River rafting trip. If you're lucky you might spot some of the park's rare animals: the bald eagle, Mexican spotted owl, desert tortoise, and mountain lion.

Dangers to the Park

Sometimes it is hard to take in the beautiful views because of the smog—a haze of air pollution—that hangs over the canyon. Winds blow pollution from a power plant fifty miles away, and the exhaust from the over five million cars bringing visitors each year also hurt the air quality.

There is now a dam in the river that prevents huge spring floods, but this has changed the water temperature. Now it never gets above fifty degrees, which is too cold for the eggs of some fish that live in the river to survive. The people that manage the park, nature organizations, and the government are working on solutions to improve air quality and preserve wildlife.

▼ *Horseback riding along the Grand Canyon*

Mike's Travel Journal in North America

Can you find me in the photos?

Uptown, Downtown

The French-Canadian city of Quebec is almost 400 years old, making it one of the oldest cities in North America. It's also the only city in North America that has an outdoor elevator to take you from uptown to downtown! Part of Quebec --the upper town-- sits high on a bluff. At the foot of the steep bluff is the lower town. Running up and down between them is a cable-car elevator.

Quebec, Canada

Ice Skating to School

The Rideau Canal runs through many towns in southeastern Ontario. This manmade waterway connects the Ottawa and St. Lawrence Rivers. It flows right through the center of Ottawa. In winter it freezes solid, making it the longest skating rink in the world. Some kids use it to get back and forth to school.

Ottawa, Canada

Polar Bear Crossing

Coming face to face with a polar bear could be a bit scary. What about facing up to 1,200 of the big white critters? Each fall more than a thousand polar bears hang out in Canada's tiny town of Churchill. That's about the same number of bears as people who live there! The bears gather right in the town, on Hudson Bay, waiting for the water to freeze so they can travel on the ice back to the Arctic, where they hunt seals.

Canada

Cleveland Rocks!

Rock 'n Roll music got its name in the United States city of Cleveland, Ohio. So it's natural that that's where you would find the Rock 'n Roll Hall of Fame. The building looks like an old-fashioned record player. Visitors can see collections that include: famous record albums, guitars, drums, and other instruments from famous bands, costumes, photos of stars, and lots of other stuff related to rock 'n roll. The Hall of Fame displays everything from one of the Beatles' reports cards to another famous star's Scout uniform.

Ohio, USA

Standing Tall in Northern California

Giant Sequoia trees grow on the western slopes of the Sierra Nevada Mountains. Not only are they tall--some reach 300 feet--but some are thought to be the oldest living things on earth. We're talking more than 3,000 years old and still growing!

Nevada, USA

Miss Liberty

Many Americans consider this statue to be a symbol of their belief in freedom. The full name of the statue is "Liberty Enlightening the World." Americans know it as the Statue of Liberty. Designed by a French sculptor, the statue (which bears the face of the sculptor's mother!) was given to the United States by the people of France in 1886. It stands in New York harbor. For many years, immigrants coming to the United States from Europe, Africa, or South America arrived in New York by ship, and the Statue of Liberty was the first "face" they saw welcoming them to their new country.

New York, USA

189

If You Lived Here

Home, community, food, school, fun, celebrations, places to visit, and more! Kids all around the world have so many common experiences. Here's how kids in North America might enjoy a few more things familiar to many kids around the globe—as well as a peek at some unique events!

Happy Birthday!

In Newfoundland, Nova Scotia, and Prince Edward Island in **Canada**, on your birthday somebody greases your nose with a dab of butter or oil! That's to help you slide past any bad luck in the year to come!

Most people in **Canada** and the **United States** celebrate a birthday with a cake decorated with candles. There is a candle for every year and often one extra one "to grow on." Everybody sings "Happy Birthday," which was written more than 100 years ago by two sisters in the United States. It is such a simple melody that today people around the world sing the same song in their own languages. In Quebec, Canada, many people sing it in French.

Now I'll do a little birthday dance!

What an Event!

Ayiee! Jumping is easy!

Things are really jumping at the Calaveras County Jumping Frog Contest in California. The frog with the longest single hop wins. The record is more than 20 feet.

Every July a hot-dog eating contest is held at the beach in Coney Island, New York. Who ever eats the most hot dogs and buns in 12 minutes wins. The record is more than 50 hot-dogs!

The Family Pet

In the **United States** cats and dogs fight it out for the honor of most popular pet, with over 60 million of each in households across the country. Birds, fish, and small rodents like gerbils, guinea pigs and hamsters are also popular.

I could be popular, too, don't you think?

In **Canada**, dogs, cats, and small birds are the most popular pets. But in the far north, Native American Inuit kids sometimes tame wild foxes, birds, and even baby seals.

Glossary

Afrikaaner: South Africans of Dutch ethnicity

Banderilleros: in Spanish bullfighting, people who jab the bull's back with pointed sticks

Sevillana: traditional Spanish folk dance

Abaya: long cotton gown worn in public by Saudi Arabian girls ages 9 and up

Ayo: popular Nigerian board game

Baobab: national tree of Senegal

Barrio: Costa Rican city neighborhood

Basarwa: first people in South Africa

Bonsai: Japanese art of trimming and pruning trees to stay small but appear full grown

Capoeira: Brazilian kick-fighting sport that started 400 years ago.

Cesta: handwoven, curved basket used by jai alai players

Chisanbop: South Korean method of arithmetic using the fingers of the right hand to stand for numbers from one to nine and fingers of the left hand to stand for tens.

Chun Jie: Chinese New Year in Singapore

Chusok: South Korea's thanksgiving holiday

Diwali: Indian autumn festival of lights

Durbar: a Nigerian display of horsemanship during a celebration

Eid al-Fitr: feast celebrating the end of Ramadan, an important Muslim holiday

Ejido: small Mexican farm

Escuelita: small Peruvian village school

Estancia: large Argentine farm or ranch

Flamenco: traditional Spanish folk dance

Fourth of July: Independence Day in the United States

Gaucho: Argentine cowboy working on a farm

Halloween: United States celebration on the eve of All Saints' Day, usually involving costumes and candy

Hamites: Egyptians who can trace their roots back to the time of Abraham in the Bible

Hanbok: short jacket worn over a long full skirt (women and girls) or draped pants (boys and men) during South Korea's thanksgiving holiday

Harmattan: a hot wind that blows from the Sahara Desert during the dry season in Nigeria

Hijab: Iranian scarf worn to cover a girl's hair in public

Holi: Indian spring-cleaning festival

Hutong: traditional Chinese homes, grouped around a central courtyard

Jai alai: handball played with a handwoven, curved basket called a cesta, popular in Mexico and elsewhere

Jamhuri: Kenyan Independence Day

Jota: traditional Spanish folk dance

Kabbadi: ancient Indian sport of tag still played today

Kendo: ancient Japanese form of fencing using wooden and bamboo swords

Khaneh Tekani: literally "shaking the house," an the Iranian tradition of cleaning the house for New Years'

Ludo: popular Nigerian board game

Mariachi: Mexican street band

Matadors: Spanish bullfighters

Matkot: Israeli game that is a cross between tennis and paddleball

Mech gumi: Nepalese circle game

Mekes: Fijian dance ceremonies that tell a story with movement

Meseta: high plateau at the center of Spain

Moulid: Egyptian feast days for Muslim and Christian holidays, including a street fair, market, and amusement park

Noruz: Iranian New Year celebration.

Palio: annual horse race in Siena, Italy, over 900 years old

Panjat Pinang: Indonesian palm-tree-climbing contest, with prizes hung from the top of a greased tree trunk

Pato: Argentine sport where players on horseback try to get a six-handled ball into a high basket

Pencak Silat: Indonesian fighting sport resembling judo or karate

Ramadan: monthlong Muslim holiday, marked by fasting between sunup and sundown by everyone age thirteen and up

Sapo: Peruvian board game, probably invented by Spanish settlers

Sheshbesh: Israeli board game similar to backgammon

Singlish: Singaporean slang, combining English, Malay, Tamil, and Mandarin words

Songkran: Thailand's New Year

Souk: Arabian marketplace

Sumo: Japanese style of wrestling

Tamkharit: Senegalese celebration of the Muslim New Year

Tihar: Nepalese fall festival celebrated by Hindus

Tope: Costa Rican pre-Christmas parade

Trulli: round white houses with cone-shaped roofs made of layered stones, found on the southeast coast of Italy

Wolof: largest ethnic group in Senegal

Yunza: Peruvian harvest festival

Now it's time to say goodbye!

This is how the children of our world say it!

Zài jiàn
Chinese

Na shledanou
Czech

Ahn nyung hee gyae se yo
Korean

Phir milengay
Hindi

Andio
Greek

Au revoir
French

Auf Wiedersehen
German

Selamat tinggal
Indonesian and Malay

Arrivederci
Italian

Lehitraot
Hebrew

Index

Photo Credits

Front Cover: Lissac/Hoaqui – Sunset – Corbis – Corbis – Troncy/Hoaqui – Bruce Clarke – Getty – Getty
Back Cover: Tiedeman/Corbis – Su/Corbis – Colin/Hemisphères – Harryhausen/Alamy
p 6: Getty – Nicolas/Hemispheres, p 7: Sunset – Corbis – Getty, p 8: Welcome to Our World: Lissac/Hoaqui – Bartruff/Corbis – Bartruff/Corbis – Sunset – Corbis Sunset – Getty – Nicolas/Hemispheres – Getty – Sunset – Corbis, p 9: Who We Are: Nowitz/Corbis – Getty, p 10: Where We Live: Alamy – Corbis, p 11: Our Communities: Bringard/Hemispheres – Torrione/Hemispheres, What We Eat: Grandadam/Hoaqui, p 12: What We Study: Getty Image Bank, What We Do for Fun: Getty/ImageBank – Alamy, p 13: Holidays & Celebrations: Lees/Getty – Getty, p 14: Taking Care of Our World: Alamy – Alamy – Amet/Corbis

Africa, Map, p 15: Let's Explore Africa: Hugues/Hemisphères, The People: Getty, p 17: The Animals: Getty Egypt, p 18: Lenars/Corbis, p 19: Who We Are: Nowitz/Corbis, Our Country: Getty, Our Communities: Getty Stone, p 20: What We Eat: Hoaqui, What We Study: Peterson/Corbis, What We Do for Fun: Hoaqui, p 21: Holidays & Celebrations: Vaninni/Corbis, Mystery Builders: Getty Kenya, p 22: Lissac/ Hoaqui, p 23: Who We Are: D.R, Our Country: Getty, Our Communities: Robert Harding/Alamy, p 24: What We Eat: Hoaqui, What We Study: Davies/Corbis, What We Do for Fun: Arthus–Bertrand/ Corbis, p 25: Holidays & Celebrations: Hoaqui, Animal Migration: Getty Nigeria, p 26: Huet/Hoaqui, p 27: Who We Are: Huet/Hoaqui, Our Country: Perousse/Hoaqui, Our Communities: Corbis, p 28: What We Eat: Almasy/Corbis, What We Study: Huet/Hoaqui, What We Do for Fun: Tiedeman/Corbis, p 29: Holidays & Celebrations: Renaudeau/Hoaqui – Renaudeau/Hoaqui, Oil and the Environnement: Huet/Hoaqui Senegal, p 30: Frances/Hemispheres, p 31: Who Are We: Nicolas/Hemispheres, Our Country: Arthus–Bertrand/Corbis, Our Communities: Vaninni/Corbis, p 32: What We Eat: Frilet/Hemispheres, What We Study: Sunset, What We Do for Fun: Franck/Corbis, p 33: Holidays & Celebrations: List/Corbis, Upside Down Tree: Dennis/Gallo Images/Corbis South Africa, p 34: Getty, p 35: Who Are We: Getty/Taxi, Our Country: Royalty-free, Our Communities: Royalty-free, p 36: What We Eat: Heeb/Hemispheres, What We Study: Evrard/Alamy What We Do for Fun: Frances/Hemispheres, p 37: Holidays & Celebrations: Bruce Clarke, National Parks: Corbis – Getty, Mike's travel journal, Carte 11741, aut. n°0505212, © Michelin et Cie, 2005, p 38: Getty – Corbis – Alamy, p 39: Alamy – Corbis – Alamy

Asia & Oceania, Map, p 41: Let's Explore Asia: Slick Shoots/Alamy, The People: Getty Stone, p 43: The Animals: Getty Taxi, The Environment: Getty Stone - Getty Stone China, p 44: Nicolas/Hemispheres, p 45: Who Are We: Getty Stone, Our Country: Reflet/Explorer/Hoaqui, Our Communities: le Flo'ch/ Hoaqui, p 46: What We Eat: Kaestner/Corbis, What We Study: Grandadam/Hoaqui, What We Do for Fun: BNPM/Corbis, p 47: Holidays & Celebrations: Su/Corbis – Su/Corbis, Open Topic: Getty Stone India, p 48: Getty, p 49: Who Are We: Getty Stone, Our Country: Alamy, Our Communities: Corbis, p 50: What We Eat: Hill/Cephas Photo lib./Alamy, What We Study: Wells/Corbis, What We Do for Fun: Lisle/Corbis, p 51: Holidays & Celebrations: Soltan/Hoaqui – Alamy, Monsoon: Getty Stone Indonesia, p 52: Corbis, p 53: Who Are We: Getty Stone, Our Country: Alamy, Our Communities: Alamy, p 54: What We Eat: AskImages, What We Study: Alamy, What We Do for Fun: Alamy – Getty, p 55: Holidays & Celebrations: Alamy, Loosing The Forest: Alamy Iran, p 56: Wojtek/Hoaqui, p 57: Who Are We: Gellie/Hoaqui, Our Country: Harney/Alamy, Our Communities: Bruno Morandi, p 58: What We Eat: Kowall/Corbis, What We Study: Colin/Hemispheres, What We Do for Fun: Bruno Morandi, p 59: Holidays & Celebrations: Alamy, Colored tiles: Wojtek/Hoaqui Israel, p 60: Corbis, p 61: Who Are We: Alamy, Our Country: Sioen/Hoaqui, Our Communities: Attal/Ask Images, p 62: What We Eat: Nicolas/Hemisphere, What We Study: Corbis, What We Do for Fun: Alamy, p 63: Holidays & Celebrations: Alamy – Alamy, Dead Sea: Nowitz/Corbis Japan, p 64: Mcvay/Getty Image, p 65: Who Are We: Getty/Image Bank, Our Country: Getty Stone, Our Communities: Getty, p 66: What We Eat: Getty/Image Bank, What We Study: Getty Stone, What We Do for Fun: Getty/Image Bank, p 67: Holidays & Celebrations: Getty Stone – Alamy, Landscape in a bowl: Yamashita/Corbis – Fields/Corbis Nepal, p 68: McDuff Everton/Corbis, p 69: Who Are We: Getty Stone, Our Country: Monteath/Hoaqui, Our Communities: Van Hasselt/Corbis, p 70: What We Eat: Alamy, What We Study: Hoaqui, What We Do for Fun: Getty Stone, p 71: Holidays & Celebrations: Bruno Morandi, Snow leopards: Alamy Saudi Arabia, p 72: Kaehler/Corbis, p 73: Who Are We: Photo Researchers/Hoaqui, Our Country: Gerard/Hoaqui, Our Communities: Getty/National Geographic, p 74: What We Eat: Explorer/Hoaqui, What We Study: Bernard/Hoaqui, What We Do for Fun: Addario/Corbis, p 75: Holidays & Celebrations: Getty Stone, Pipelines: Getty Stone Singapore, p 76: Hollingsworth/Corbis, p 77: Who Are We: Evrard/Hoaqui, Our Country: Ball/Corbis, Our Communities: Barbier/Hemispheres, p 78: What We Eat: Sinibaldi/Corbis, What We Study: Colin/Hemispheres, What We Do for Fun: Colin/Hemispheres, p 79: Holidays & Celebrations: Alamy, Container Ports: Getty Stone South Korea, p 80: Kaehler/Corbis, p 81: Who Are We: Alamy, Our Country: Getty/Image Bank, Our Communities: Azoury/Corbis, p 82: What We Eat: Alamy, What We Study: Alamy, What We Do for Fun: Alamy, p 83: Holidays & Celebrations: Alamy, Water Deer: Sunset/FLPA – Sunset/FLPA Thailand, p 84: Troncy/Hoaqui, p 85: Who Are We: Sunset, Our Country: Boisvieux/Hoaqui, Our Communities: Royalty-free, p 86: What We Eat: Royalty-free, What We Study: Lissac/Hoaqui, What We Do for Fun: Mattes/Hoaqui, p 87: Holidays & Celebrations: Alamy, Disappearing Elephants: Royalty-free Turkey, p 88: Widstrand/Corbis, p 89: Who Are We: Le Tourneur/Hoaqui, Our Country: Valentin/Hoaqui, Our Communities: Carteret/Hoaqui, p 90: What We Eat: Thibaut/Hoaqui, What We Study: Explorer/Hoaqui, What We Do for Fun: Getty/Image Bank, p 91: Holidays & Celebrations: Bruno Morandi, Pamukkale: Bruno Morandi OCEANIA, p 92: Getty – Getty, p 93: Getty – Getty – Getty Australia, p 94: Getty, p 95: Who Are We: Corbis, Our Country: Jansson/Alamy, Our Communities: Alamy, p 96: What We Eat: Getty, What We Study: Souders/Corbis, What We Do for Fun: Hoaqui, p 97: Holidays & Celebrations: Lenars/Auscape, Open Topic: Getty/Image Bank Fiji, p 98: Corbis, p 99: Who Are We: Valentin/Hoaqui, Our Country: Getty, Our Communities: Alamy, p 100: What We Eat: Alamy, What We Study: Leroux/ Explorer/Hoaqui, What We Do for Fun: Blondeau/Photo&Co/Corbis, p 101: Holidays & Celebrations: Alamy, Coral: Getty Stone Mike's Travel Journal, Carte 11751, aut. n°0505212, © Michelin et Cie, 2005, p 102: AP/Sipa – Wheeler/Corbis – Alamy – D.R., p 103: Rooney/Corbis – Corbis

Europe, Map, p 105: Let's Explore Europe: Alamy – Getty, p 107: Polking/Corbis – Getty, Czech Republic, p 108: Heaton/Alamy, p 109: Who Are We: Getty Stone, Our Country: Taylor/Corbis, Our Communities: Hoaqui, p 110: What We Eat: AskImages/Anzenberger, What We Study: Krist/Corbisov, What We Do for Fun: Corbis, p 111: Holidays & Celebrations: Turnley/Corbis, Bad Air Days: Garanger/Corbis France, p 112: Guion, p 113: Who Are We: Getty, Our Country: Guy/Imagefrance.com, Our Communities: Hoaqui, p 114: What We Eat: Getty Stone, What We Study: Felix/Imagefrance.com, What We Do for Fun: Imagefrance.com, p 115: Holidays & Celebrations: Corbis, Mont St Michel: Getty/Image Bank Germany, p 116: Sunset, p 117: Who Are We: Getty/Taxi, Our Country: Getty Stone, Our Communities: Juno/Corbis, p 118: What We Eat: Pompe/Hemispheres, What We Study: Alamy, What We Do for Fun: Kashi/Corbis, p 119: Holidays & Celebrations: Getty/ImageBank, Berlin Wall: Alamy – AskImages Greece, p 120: Getty, p 121: Who Are We: Bartruff/Corbis, Our Country: Getty Stone, Our Communities: Henley/Corbis, p 122: What We Eat: Getty/Foodpix/Sunset, What We Study: Alamy, What We Do for Fun: Carmona/Corbis, p 123: Holidays & Celebrations: Getty/Image Bank, Windmill: Getty/Image Bank Italy, p 124: Sunset, p 125: Who Are We: Renault/Hemispheres, Our Country: Wysocki/Hemispheres, Our Communities: Frazier/Alamy, p 126: What We Eat: Getty Stone, What We Study: Getty Stone, What We Do for Fun: Weatherly/Corbis, p 127: Holidays & Celebrations: Franken/Corbis, Letting Off Steam: Getty Russia, p 128: Hoaqui, p 129: Who Are We: Getty Stone, Our Country: Mattes/Explorer/Hoaqui, Our Communities: Alamy, p 130: What We Eat: Alamy, What We Study: Mendel/Corbis, What We Do for Fun: Karine/Corbis/Sygma, p 131: Holidays & Celebrations: Bartruff/Corbis, Amur Tiger: Getty/National Geographic Spain, p 132: Sunset, p 133: Who Are We: Getty Taxi, Our Country: Anzenberger/AskImages, Our Communities: Sunset, p 134: What We Eat: Parrault/Ask Images, What We Study: Getty Stone, What We Do for Fun: Wojtek/Hoaqui, p 135: Holidays & Celebrations: Fuste Raga/Corbis, Bullfighting: Sunset Sweden, p 136: Sunset, p 137: Who Are We: Getty/Image Bank, Our Country: Getty Stone, Our Communities: Sunset, p 138: What We Eat: Everton/Corbis, What We Study: Alamy, What We Do for Fun: Getty, p 139: Holidays & Celebrations: Alamy - Rabouan/Fiori/Hemispheres, Northern Light: Schafer/Corbis United Kingdom, p 140: Bartruff/Corbis , p 141: Who Are We: Chapman/Alamy, Our Country: Cavalier/Sunset, Our Communities: Getty Stone, p 142: What We Eat: Alamy, What We Study: Getty Stone, What We Do for Fun: Wysocki/Hemispheres, p 143: Holidays & Celebrations: Wysocki/Hemispheres, Open Topic: Getty/Image Bank Mike's Travel Journal: Carte 11734, aut. n°0505212, © Michelin et Cie, 2005, p 144: Getty – Alamy – Getty, p 145: Corbis – Hoaqui – Hemisphere

Latin America, Map, p 147: Let's Explore Latin America: Getty – Getty, p 149: Getty Argentina, p 150: Sunset, p 151: Who Are We: Getty, Our Country: Photographer's Choice/Getty, Our Communities: Alamy, p 152: What We Eat: Getty Stone, What We Study: Alamy, What We Do for Fun: Getty Stone, p 153: Holidays & Celebrations: Stadler/Corbis, Over the Top, Falls: Alamy Brazil, p 154: Corbis, p 155: Who Are We: De Wilde/Hoaqui, Our Country: Perousse/Hoaqui, Our Communities: Hoaqui, p 156: What We Eat: Hoaqui, What We Study: Hoaqui – De Wilde/Hoaqui, What We Do for Fun: De Wilde/Hoaqui, p 157: Holidays & Celebrations: Hoaqui, Living Large in Amazon: Lacz/Sunset Costa Rica, p 158: Rogers/Corbis, p 159: Who Are We: Harryhausen/Alamy, Our Country: Frances/Hemispheres, Our Communities: Boutin/Hoaqui, p 160: What We Eat: Getty/Foodpix, What We Study: Frances/ Hemispheres, What We Do for Fun: Rogers/Corbis, p 161: Holidays & Celebrations: Sanger/Alamy, Look Out Below!: Getty Taxi – Frances/Hemispheres Mexico, p 162: Getty Taxi, p 163: Who Are We: Frances/Hemispheres, Our Country: Getty/Image Bank, Our Communities: Lehman/Corbis, p 164: What We Eat: Wheeler/Corbis, What We Study: Getty Taxi, What We Do for Fun: Getty/Image Bank – Alamy, p 165: Holidays & Celebrations: Hebberd/Corbis, Mystery of the Pyramid: Hugues/Hemispheres Peru, p 166: Getty Taxi, p 167: Who Are We: Getty/Image Bank, Our Country: Getty Stone, Our Communities: Getty Taxi, p 168: What We Eat: Alamy, What We Study: Le Flo'ch/Hoaqui, What We Do for Fun: Reffet/Hoaqui, p 169: Holidays & Celebrations: Gohier/Hoaqui, Stargazing Peak: Alamy, Mike's Travel Journal: Carte 11212, aut. n°0505212, © Michelin et Cie, 2005, p 170: Corbis – Getty – Getty, p 171: Getty – Getty/ImageBank

North America, Map, p 173: Sunset – Getty, p 175: Moreno/Hoaqui – Corbis Canada, p 176: Getty, p 177: Who Are We: Alamy, Our Country: Yanagi/AGE/Hoaqui, Our Communities: Getty, p 178: What We Eat: Purcell/Corbis, What We Study: Alamy, What We Do for Fun: Alamy, p 179: Holidays & Celebrations: Alamy, Fish Tale: Alamy USA, p 180: Sunset/Zephyr Images, p 181: Who Are We: Getty/National Geographic, People Today: Obermann/Corbis, p 182: Our Country: Hallinan/Alamy, The Land: Getty/Image Bank, Over the Map: Getty, p 183: Lifestyle: Corbis, Old Neighborhood: Jenny/Alamy, p 184: What We Eat: Getty Taxi, What We Study: Cozad/Corbis, p 185: What We Do for Fun: Getty Stone, Sports Galore: Getty Taxi, Family Fun: Mirer/Corbis, p 186: Holidays & Celebrations: Kraft/Corbis, Fourth of July: Skelley/Corbis, Thanksgiving: Skelley/Corbis, p 187: Grand Balancing Act: Getty/Image Bank – Getty Mike's travel Journal, Carte 11212, aut. n°0505212, © Michelin et Cie, 2005, p 188: Alamy – Alamy – Corbis, p 189: Corbis – Getty – Getty

Cultural Consultants: Mehmet Acikalin, Cemalettin Ayas, Elvan Gunel, Jennifer Nichols, Beatriz Alvarado, Timothy M Dove, Annett Jurkutat-Swartz, Aleksandr Kvasov, William K. Wolf, Gaolekwe Ndwapi, Masataka Kasai, Sung Choon Park, Jui-min Tsai, Jyotsna Nanda

The following people have collaborated in the making of this book:
Sylvie Basdevant-Suzuki, April Dahlberg, Elsa Duval, François Egret, Eric Elzière, Ghislain Garcia, François Guion, Solange Lemoine, Marie-Hélène Westphalen